DIRTY LITTLE SINNER

SINNERS WELCOME

SAMANTHA BARRETT

You dirty little whore...
You knew when you picked this up that it's pure
smut.
Good girl...
Now be a good little slut and turn the page and get
ready to run through the circus while we chase you,
you Dirty Little Sinner.

ONE
MADDISON

I'm sitting in a cell again because my mother is a *piece of shit!*

This isn't the first, second or third fucking time I have been arrested because of her. Joanne Leigh is a selfish bitch who uses everyone and milks them for every cent they are worth. I thought she might have been changing for the better a couple of years back when she married Derek but I was a fucking fool. All she saw was dollar signs when she looked at him. Derek was great until I fucked things up. I blame that slimy piece of shit Cameron for ruining my life.

"Leigh." I sit up on the metal cot and look over at the officer who stands outside the metal bars of my cell.

"Yeah?"

"Your bail has been posted, let's go." Shock slams into me with the weight of a freight train.

"How? I don't have any money and no one I know has a few grand lying around to get me out of here," I blurt out. I haven't even made my phone call to let anyone know where the fuck I am.

"Don't know, don't care. Get up, you're out of here." Shocked or not, I get to my feet and practically run out of the cell the moment it's open. I don't know what the fuck is going on but I won't question it in case they made a mistake and let the wrong Leigh out.

I sign all the forms and agree to them coming to the designated address on the form to check to make sure I am home between certain hours. Thanks to my fucking mother I am now on house arrest until my court date. I've learned there is no point in trying to convince them that it wasn't me who committed the crime, they never believe me and trying to find my mother to force her to take accountability is like trying to find a needle in a haystack. I bite my tongue to keep from lashing out at the officer. This is bullshit and unfair but it's nothing I'm not used to.

If I'm not being arrested for her, then I have her dealers coming to my door and demanding I pay up or they will take their payment in other forms. I was careful this time. When I packed my shit and moved out of Derek's I never told a soul where I lived... wait. I bumped into Joanne's best friend Scarlet a couple of weeks back, that little bitch! She must have followed me and ratted me out to Joanne!

Fuck!

I snatch the paper bag off the counter, filled with my meager belongings that I had on me, and stalk out of there. I'm tired, hungry and pissed the hell off and all I want to do is climb into my bed and sleep for the next week. I push the door open and inhale the fresh air, the smell of freedom is intoxicating. I close my eyes and just take a minute to be. I know it will only be a matter of time before something else pops up from Joanne so I'll have to move.

"Well, don't you just look edible, *little sinner.*" Ice fills my veins and my heart skips a beat at the sound of his voice. I snap my eyes open and the image of Cameron leaning against his truck is the sight of a nightmare. The bastard has the balls to stand there smiling up at me like he isn't the reason that my life was turned upside down after finally planting some roots and being free of my mother. He ruined everything.

"What the fuck are you doing here, Cameron?"

My voice is filled with malice but the asshole either doesn't notice or just chooses to ignore it.

"Coming to rescue you, of course. Now, are you going to be a good girl and get in the truck, or are you going to do things the hard way and make me chase you?"

I'm blaming the fact I haven't been fucked in almost a year for the way my body responds to his taunt. Need coils low in my belly and want thrums through me as a memory of the night he wore a mask and chased me through the carnival after it closed assaults me.

"I don't owe you shit and I sure as fuck am not going anywhere with you," I hiss as I make my way down the steps. I try to walk past him but the motherfucker darts in front of me, blocking my path, causing me to collide with his hard chest. I stumble back a step and would have fallen but Cameron grips my waist and heat instantly unfurls inside me at having his hands on me again. Before I can get too lost in my own traitorous thoughts, I bat his hands away and take a step back. "Leave me alone," I grit out through clenched teeth.

"Little sinner, you don't have a choice," he breathes out with a hint of annoyance in his tone, which just pisses me off. He has no right to be pissy when he is the reason for this mess. If he didn't trick me I would have still been living with him, Derek and Royce.

"Fuck you. I'm going home—"

"Your stuff is in my truck. I stopped by your place on the way and caught your mother's *friends* ransacking your place." I open my mouth to argue and find out how he even knew where the fuck I live but he pushes on. "Your terms of bail are to remain at the address you agreed to and it just so happens I switched that address to ours." My jaw unhinges as I gape up at him. "In the truck, sinner, we have a long drive and I want to get home as soon as we can."

Cam leaves me standing on the sidewalk as he makes his way to his truck, my mind whirling. If what he said is true and Joanne's people were going through my place, then it isn't safe to go back there. Plus, if I breach my bail terms, I will just end up back in a fucking cell!

I growl out my frustration and stomp my ass back to his truck. Cam grins at me when I slide in beside him but I ignore the asshole. Going back to his house is the last thing I want to do, not after what happened. I push that thought from my mind and force myself to think about anything else as Cam drives us back to his place. I watch the buildings blur as I get lost in my own thoughts. I avoid thinking too much because my thoughts always end up back on those three and it's wrong—I shouldn't be thinking about them like that, especially my stepfather.

Derek Vought.

Cam is the polar opposite of his father—Derek is stern and all business. He runs his business and household with an iron fist, craves control and submission from everyone except his son and brother. Royce may not be related to the both of them by blood, but Derek and him have always referred to each other as brothers. Joanne wouldn't be someone I would have picked to end up with Derek and honestly, I have no idea what he saw in her. After three weeks of dating they were engaged, then six weeks later they were married. The marriage lasted about five months before she took off and left me behind. I didn't care though because I had Cam, Royce and Derek.

Cam and I used to sneak around all the time and fuck. There is no denying Cameron is fucking sexy with his emo jock look. Blond hair just long enough to run your fingers through, striking blue eyes that see through you and tattoos that cover every inch of his body. He may look like a jokester and be carefree but the moment you are alone and naked with him, a whole other side comes out and the devil in him is unleashed. I still recall the night I found him and Royce together. Fuck, the sight of them both naked and groaning had me soaking my panties in seconds.

I shiver as I remember the way he felt moving inside me. Cam took me anywhere and anytime he wanted. I was powerless against the need I felt for him. I craved him more than air but I can't lie and say I wasn't attracted to Royce and Derek. I managed to control my want toward them until the night I got caught sucking my stepdad's cock by his brother and son.

Maddy hasn't spoken a word since she climbed in the truck. I know she's lost in her own head so I leave her be when all I really want to do is reach across and trail my hand up the inside of her thighs until she's squirming and begging for me to take her. God, the sounds she would make as I slid inside her tight little cunt have haunted me since the moment she left us.

She didn't just destroy me when she left, Dad and Royce were devastated over the loss of her too. She thinks I have no idea that she was into my dad and uncle, but the truth is, I knew and I fucking loved it. We live a different type of life style to most people. We own a circus and carnival and set up a home base about five years ago. We make a damn good living from it and I know Maddison loved it as much as we do. Her mother was a gold digging whore who only married my dad because she thought she could get her claws into our money, but he isn't stupid and had her sign a prenup.

When Joanne realized she wasn't getting a cent from him, she took off and left her daughter behind without a second thought. Maddy thinks we had no idea where she has been but the truth is, we have been tracking her the entire time. Royce, Dad and I have been taking turns keeping an eye on her. Tonight seeing her get arrested because of that cunt of a mother of hers forced my hand. I cleared her shitty apartment out and packed her things, then bailed her ass out because it's time she gets her ass home where she belongs.

"How did you find me, Cam?" she asks quietly. The hint of defeat I hear in her voice has me gripping the steering wheel in a death grip.

"You were never missing, sinner. There is no need to find something that isn't lost."

"What the hell does that mean?" I smirk at the bite in her tone, there's the spitfire I know and love.

"It means we have known where you have been this entire time." I glance over at her and smirk at the wide eyed look on her face. Her mouth parts and I bite back a groan. "Close that mouth before I fill it with my dick."

She clamps her mouth closed and scowls at me. "You'll never touch me again."

I chuckle. "You and I both know that you are full of shit. You missed my cock as much as it missed your sweet cunt."

"No, the fuck, I didn't," she snaps.

"God knows you are lying, baby."

"Don't call me that."

"Whatever you say, my dirty little sinner."

"Stop it, Cameron. I mean it." I would believe her if it wasn't for the note of need lining her warning, so I decide to push her.

"So do I. I miss the feeling of those beautiful full lips wrapped around me while I fuck your throat. I still think about that time I chased you through the maze in a mask and cornered you—"

"Stop!"

"Why?" I fight back.

"Because that was a long time ago and it was wrong. For fuck's sake, Cam, our parents are still married. You're my stepbrother—"

"Didn't stop you from riding my cock on the ferris wheel now, did it?" She inhales sharply. I chance a glance at her and smirk. Her green eyes are shooting fireballs, her black hair loose and begging for me to tangle my fingers in the strands and yank hard as I slam into her.

"Didn't stop you from setting me up!" she shouts, then crosses her arms over her chest and slouches back into her seat.

I sigh and shake my head. "I never set you up, Maddison." At the use of her real name she slowly turns and faces me. I turn and look directly at her so she can see the truth in my eyes.

"Who did?" she breathes out.

"No one. It was an accident. I had every intention of meeting you in the office that night. In fact, I was on my way to you when Royce intercepted me and told me we had an issue with the bumper cars. I thought I would have time to help him then come back and meet you..." I let my sentence trail off when I see the cogs whirling in her head.

"Wait. So that means your father..." Her eyes widen and her mouth falls open as understanding slams into her.

I shoot my sinner a grin. "He knew it was you and never stopped you because he wanted you as much as you wanted him."

Maddy turns pale as she shakes her head. "No, I never looked at him or Royce—"

"Who said anything about Royce?" I hedge. She opens and closes her mouth a few times but no words come out. It may be dark in the cab of the truck but I know without needing to see her clearly that her cheeks are tinged red. I know she is thinking about the time she caught me and Royce fucking in the living room. Royce isn't my uncle by blood. Him and Dad just tell people they are brothers and thank fuck for that, because I love burying my cock in his ass. "You think I didn't know that you wanted my dad and uncle?" The gasp that escapes her has a sinister chuckle escaping me. "Oh, my sinner, we all knew you wanted the three of us. Dad tried to fight against his need for you. He tried to go to church because he thought something was wrong with him, but Royce and I knew God couldn't save him because you were put on this earth to tempt the fuck out of us, baby." Not needing to hear her denial, I turn the radio up and fill the truck with a track from Rihanna.

I snort when I realize the lyrics to the song are "Kiss It Better". Fuck, I hunger to taste her on my tongue again. I fight the urge to pull the truck over and take her now. Her mouth may say she hates me, but we both know her body wants me and I would bet good fucking money that she is wet right now.

The rest of the drive is spent in silence. I should

have text or called to give Dad and Royce a heads up that she was coming back with me, but I didn't have a second to think, so they are in for a surprise when we get home. Royce may never have had a chance to touch Maddy or even taste her, but I know that didn't stop him from picturing her beneath him and how sweet she would taste on his tongue.

Dad, on the other hand, did get to touch her and ever since that night he hasn't been the same. He thought I didn't know he was into her but the man couldn't play a game of poker to save his life. He's easy as shit to read. Seeing her on her knees with my dad's dick down her throat was one of the hottest things I have ever seen in my life. Just the thought of seeing her take Royce, Dad and me at once has me wanting to bust a nut in my pants like some weak teenage boy who can't last longer than two pumps.

It takes another two hours before we finally make it back home. As we roll down the private road, the lights of the carnival can be seen. I look over at her and see a ghost of a smile on her lips. She may never admit it but I know for a fact she loved living out here and being a part of the business. She was a huge reason why we chose not to let the animals live in cages and bought the surrounding land around us, so they could have better space and be able to live with a bit more freedom. We only take in animals that can't be returned to the wild or who have been rescued from homes.

Maddy loved spending time with the lions and tigers. Surprisingly, we have one lion who no one can get near except for her. Hades is a pure white lion with anger issues. Maddy didn't know he was dangerous and one day when I went looking for her I found her out in the pasture with him. He was like a puppy dog with her, but the moment he spotted me he went ape shit but he never turned on her. As we passed the pastures out back, I feel her shift next to me and peer out her window looking for him.

"He was moved to the back of the property," I say.

"Why?" Her tone is laced with outrage.

"No one was able to walk past his area without him attacking the fence. We had to get the vet out to dart him and move him to the back."

"He hates being on his own, Cameron. You know this!"

"Yeah, well, I wasn't the one who left him now, was I, sinner?"

I snap my mouth shut and ignore Cam as we pull up in front of the house. It's far enough from the attractions and the huge tent that a lot of the noise doesn't reach the house. I look up at the large barndominium style house and a pang of longing hits me in the chest. This was the first place that had ever felt like home to me. I never had a home growing up. Joanne could never pay the rent on time, so we couch surfed all my life. I never went to a normal school. I was homeschooled and had to teach myself because my mother was useless or strung out of her mind, out on her three day benders with one of her numerous boyfriends.

Joanne's legs are like a revolving door, open to

anyone who wants to walk in. Derek was the first boyfriend she ever had that was kind to me. He never tried to touch me or let his gaze linger on my ass or tits. He respected me and I fucked that up. Now that I know the truth about that night, I have no idea how to feel. I ran before anyone could explain and I've never looked back since. I'm twenty-one and working part time jobs just to survive because I have no purpose in life. I thought I had found my calling, working with all the animals here, but then I left.

When Cam kills the engine, the lights inside the cab flicker on and blind me. He pushes his door open and I drop my gaze to my lap and nibble on my bottom lip nervously.

"Look at me." The dominance in his tone has my body obeying him without thought. It's always been like that with him, even if my mind was screaming for the opposite. "You belong here, with *us*." I inhale sharply as warmth spreads through me. "Get your ass out of the car and head up to your room. Royce and Dad should still be locking up. Escape to your room now while you have the chance." Cam doesn't have to tell me twice. I jump out of the car and rush to the house, pushing the door open. I don't look around to see if anything has changed, I rush up the spiral staircase and head for my old room. My room is in the middle. Cam's is the first on the right, Royce's is the second on the left, opposite mine, and Derek's room is at the end of the hall.

When I push the door open and flick the light on, I freeze in the doorway. My hand comes up and covers my mouth. The room is *exactly* as I left it. I walk in slowly and take in my surroundings. My twin bed is unmade, just like I left it. Clothes are still hung in the closet and my drawers are open with clothes spilling out of them. I was in such a rush to get out of here I grabbed what I could and ran.

"Where the hell have you been?" I whirl around at the sound of Derek's voice downstairs. Goosebumps dot my arms as I suddenly feel exposed and unsure if I should have let Cam convince me to come back here.

"You know where I have been," Cam fires back.

"Calm down, Derek. You knew he was heading to the city to watch over Maddy." Hearing Royce say my name again after so long has a dull ache forming between my legs.

Fuck, I need to get laid!

"How is she?" The concern in Derek's voice has me slowly exiting my room and heading to the railing that overlooks the downstairs of the house. My breath hitches when I take in the sight of him, Royce and Cameron standing in the open plan living room. Derek still looks good, only he could pull off a black cotton tee with black jeans and make them look like a million bucks. His black hair is a mess, strands have fallen onto his forehead and I itch to push them back. I know his blue eyes would be burning with a dangerous intensity as he waits for his son to answer him. His forearms are covered in tattoos, they are a tribute to his life. One arm is a carnival sleeve and the other is decorated in all things that represent his circus.

I grip the rail in a vice-like hold to keep myself in place. Royce moves to Cam's side, drawing my attention to him. Out of the three, he is the one who actually looks like he belongs in this place. He's wearing a pair of dark wash denim jeans, a flannel shirt tied around his waist and white shirt that is covered in bits of hay—clearly he just finished feeding the animals. Royce's black hair is cropped short on the sides and longer on the top. I always found comfort in his soft brown eyes.

Derek and Royce are both young. They are the same age with only a couple of months separating them. They're thirty-nine. Derek was eighteen when

Cameron was born. Cam's mom took off and left his father and Royce to raise him on their own, and honestly, they did a fucking amazing job. Cam is twenty-one, the same age as me, and I know he loves his father and has the utmost respect for him.

"Why don't you ask her yourself?" The sound of Cameron's voice pulls me from my thoughts. I peer down at him to find his gaze locked on to me. Derek and Royce both follow his line of sight and the moment they see me, both of their eyes widen in surprise. Silence stretches and I fight not to fidget, waiting for one of them to say something, anything to remove this awkward tension in the air.

"Sinner," Derek breathes out and I release a breath I didn't know I was holding. They all started calling me *sinner* when I befriended Hades. They said that the lion was born of the devil and the only way someone would be able to tame him is if the person was a sinner like Lucifer himself.

"Hi, Derek," I say quietly. He shudders at the sound of my voice.

"Welcome home, darling." I shoot Royce a small smile and nibble on the corner of my lip.

"Joanne got her arrested. Gave Maddison's name and address to the cops. They picked her up earlier tonight and locked her fine ass up. I bailed her out.

She's on house arrest here until her court date in a couple of weeks." All three look up at me, waiting for an explanation but I can't formulate words. The tension inside me is suffocating and Cam's words from earlier are playing on repeat.

They want you.

Was he telling the truth?

Did he just say that shit to make me feel better about sucking his dad off? All these thoughts are plaguing me and I can't focus on anything thanks to the throbbing ache between my legs. I need to get away from them and their assessing gazes.

"I need a shower," I blurt, then rush back down the hall and escape inside the bathroom. I almost whimper when I see my shampoo, conditioner and face wash still tucked neatly away in the corner of the open plan shower. This bathroom is like no other. The tub is in the corner with a large window beside it, giving a clear view of the pens out the back. I hate that it's so dark out that I can't see Hades. The shower is open and has a rainfall showerhead fixed into the roof—the bloody thing can even turn into a steamer.

I strip and toss my clothes into the hamper before turning the shower on. The second the water heats, I step under the spray and close my eyes, letting the water cascade down my body and praying it can wash away all my thoughts and wipe away the need for the three alpha males downstairs.

Sinner is the perfect name for me because I so badly want to sin with my stepbrother, stepdad and uncle.

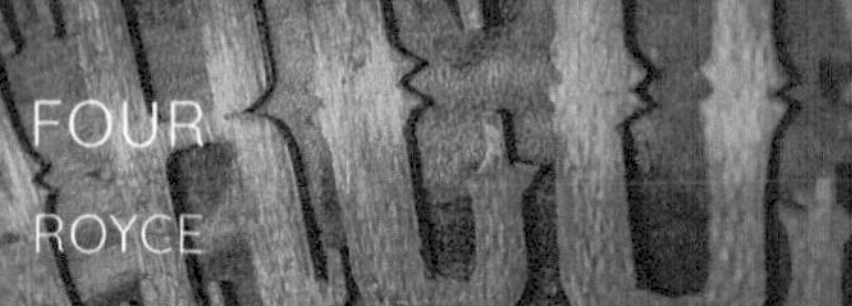

FOUR
ROYCE

"She's back," Derek mutters when Maddy disappears. Cam snorts and shakes his head as he claps his dad on the shoulder.

"Yeah, dude, and I told her the truth." My eyes widen.

"Why the fuck would you do that?" I snap.

Cam rolls his eyes and I narrow mine, telling him without words that I'll punish him later for that act of defiance. Derek is aware of me and Cam fucking, he wasn't happy about it when he found out but he knows Cam and I find pleasure in each other and that's it. We enjoy each other's body's but we aren't committed to one another.

"She was worried Dad would lose his shit after what happened. I set her straight and believe me, she still wants us even if she won't admit it." The moment we all hear the shower turn on, everyone falls silent. Derek groans and stabs a hand through his hair, pushing it back.

"Jesus, this is a clusterfuck," D bites out, then takes off toward the back door. Cameron sighs and shakes his head.

"He'll come around, give him some time," I say. Cam nods but I can tell he's worried about his old man. I open my mouth but then a scream from Maddison rends the air. Cam and I both take off toward the stairs, taking them two at a time. I'm right on his heels as he pushes the bathroom door open. The second I spot Maddison standing under the water naked, my blood heats and my cock twitches to life in my pants.

Her full tits are perky, her nipples hard and begging for me to wrap my lips around them—

"What the fuck happened?" I shake my head and push those thoughts from my mind at the sound of Cam's voice.

"There's a spider," she hisses and points out where it is. I bite back a laugh. Cam sighs and stalks forward into the shower. Maddy takes a step away from him, then locks eyes with me. Her mouth parts on a silent gasp, clearly she didn't see me standing behind Cameron. I lose the battle and my eyes glide down her wet little body. The second I make it to her pussy, I'm shoved from behind and stumble forward, slipping on some water and colliding with Maddison. She squeals in surprise as I pin her against the tiled wall.

"I heard a scream." Derek's voice is drowned out by the blood pumping in my ears, Maddison's body is pressed against me and I know she can feel how hard I am for her. Her eyes are round as she looks up at me, my breathing ragged. It's only then I realize my hands are gripping her waist—she fits against me perfectly.

"She saw a spider," Cam mutters. I turn my head and see him standing there staring at us with hunger in his eyes. My cock twitches and Maddison gasps when she feels it.

"So is this now a communal shower?" Derek grits out. I know he has his reservations about wanting her but I don't, nor does Cameron. As much as I would love to drop to my knees right this second and plunge my tongue inside her delectable pussy, I won't push her until I know for certain she wants us the same way we want her.

I push back and see a flicker of hurt flash through her eyes before she masks it, it was so brief that if I wasn't paying such close attention I would have missed it. The instant I step aside and Derek gets a look at her he hisses, then curses beneath his breath and storms down the hall. His bedroom door slams closed a moment later and Maddy's face falls.

"My room now, Cameron," I grit out as I whirl around and don't look back at her. I need relief and I need it now. I'm in my bedroom all of five seconds before Cameron appears. I grip the front of his shirt and slam him against the wall, he grunts from the force but doesn't protest as I smash my lips against his. Cam opens for me and I relish in the fact he may be a dominant motherfucker when it concerns Maddison, but he and I both know I am the one in charge when it comes to him and me.

Cam pushes his hand between our bodies and cups my dick, drawing a groan from me. I bite down on his bottom lip, loving the way his eyes burn with fire at my show of power. His hand closes around my length.

"Knees, now," I snarl as I take a step back. I untie my flannel and let it drop to the floor as Cam lowers to his knees and pops the button on my jeans, then yanks the zipper down. His movements are just as hurried as mine. Maddison has set us all on edge and unlike Derek, Cameron and I can find release from each other. The moment Cam wraps his hand around my shaft I throw my head back and groan. "Suck it," I growl as I flop my head forward and watch as his lips suction around my dick. A ripple of pleasure rolls through me as he sucks me all the way into the back of his throat. Movement from the corner of my eye catches my attention. I peer over and see Maddison standing in the hallway with her towel wrapped around her body, staring at Cameron sucking me off.

I reach down and grip his hair, pulling hard as I thrust into his mouth, loving the sound of him choking on my length. She meets my gaze and I wait to see what she will do. I challenge her with my eyes to show me what she wants. As if she can read my thoughts she turns and leans her back against her closed door and drops her towel. I growl my approval as she cups her left tit in her hand and twirls her nipple between her fingers. Then she slowly glides her right hand down her toned stomach and doesn't stop until she is cupping her pussy.

I pull free of Cam's mouth and shoot her a wink before walking over to the end of my bed so she can get a clear view as I bend over the edge. Cam chuckles and shakes his head when he spots her. He snatches the lube off my dresser, then comes to stand behind me.

"You can join anytime you want, sinner," he taunts. Her eyes burn with an intensity and I can see her debating her options.

"Tonight, I will only eat your pussy while Cam fucks me. If you're a good girl, I might fuck you tomorrow." She darts her tongue out and moistens her lips, I can see she is weighing her options. The second Cam squirts the lube onto his dick, she stalks into the room and kicks the door closed behind herself, then leans against it.

"Get your ass on the bed now and keep those fucking legs open. I want to watch him eat that cunt." Hearing the authoritative tone Cam uses with her sends a thrill of anticipation through me. I can tell she is unsure and wondering if she is making the wrong choice, but the second Cam slowly eases inside me, her need wins out. She climbs on the bed and spreads her legs like she was told. She's soaking wet, her arousal coating the inside of her thighs. I groan when Cameron buries himself balls deep inside my ass, I know he is too wound up to last long and I need the three of us to come together so I don't tease her. I bury my face in between her legs and suck her clit into my mouth.

"Fuck!" she screams out, so loud I know there is no way Derek didn't hear. I want to push my brother to the edge and force his hand. We aren't doing anything wrong and Joanne is a cunt, but in Derek's head until his divorce is complete in a few weeks he would be cheating. He owes that cunt nothing, yet he holds his vows in high regards.

"Her pussy tastes so good, doesn't it?" Cam grits out as he thrusts inside me, drawing a strangled moan of pleasure from me. I love it when he's unhinged and fucks me like a crazed man. Maddison pushes up onto her elbows and locks eyes with me as I push two fingers inside her, loving the way her eyes roll back in pleasure. I don't build her up, I would love to take my time and explore what she likes but I know the moment Cam comes she will run. I need to make sure she sees stars before that happens and pray she will crave another round with me.

"Hmmmm," I reply as I scrape my teeth along her sensitive nub.

"Holy shit," she cries out.

"You like that, sinner?" Cam asks.

She flicks her eyes to him and nods. "Yes. It feels so good."

"You gonna come on his tongue like a good little whore, baby?"

Her eyes blaze when he calls her a whore and I make a mental note about that, she loves being degraded and that shit only heightens my hunger for her.

"Fuck yes," she purrs as she grinds against my face, chasing her release. This time I will allow control but next time, she will submit to me and be given only what I allow her to have.

I try to keep my moans quiet, knowing Derek is just next door. But when Royce curls his fingers inside me and strokes my G-spot again while sucking on my clit, I lose the battle as my orgasm rips through me like a wildfire and I scream his name. I hear Cam roaring his release at the same time and that sends a shiver through me. This is the hottest sexual experience I have ever had. Royce laps at my pussy and brings me down gently, I slowly blink my eyes open when the shudders finally subside.

The moment I lock eyes with Royce, panic sets in, he pulls back instantly from the look on my face. He smiles reassuringly but it does nothing to ease the panic. Before either of them can utter a word, I leap off the bed, run out of the room and lock myself inside my own room. My heart is pounding so hard against my ribs I worry everyone will be able to hear it.

"Get a grip, you are all adults!" I hiss. I dart forward and jump on my bed, yanking the covers over my naked body and decide to hide under them until morning.

How the fuck am I going to face Royce?

I feel no awkwardness toward Cam, he and I got over that shit a long time ago, but I just let his uncle eat my pussy while his dick was buried in his ass. Fuck, images of Cam on his knees with Royce's dick in his mouth has me clenching my thighs together. I force those thoughts out of my head and scrunch my eyes closed. I need sleep, after a good night's rest, everything will be better tomorrow and I can act like nothing happened.

Okay, maybe I'm not as mature as I thought I was. I know Derek and the others all wake at around five so I made sure to be out of the house by four-thirty to avoid them. I'm not ready to face any of them after what happened last night. I've been walking around aimlessly for nearly an hour with no destination in mind. I smile when I spot the merry-go-round. I remember one night after my mom left me here, I was upset because I was jealous that Cameron had a good parent and I didn't. I said nothing to Derek but he could just tell. He brought me out here and sat behind the operator's desk and told me to ride as long as I wanted and he would wait until I was ready.

I don't know what came over me that night, but after about twenty minutes, I broke down in tears. I didn't realize the ride had stopped or that Derek's arms were wrapped around me until the tears had finally stopped. He promised me that night that he would always be there for me and he didn't need to be married to my mother to make that promise. He told me I would always hold a special place in his heart and now I wonder if he meant that in a different way?

"If you're trying to hide, you're not doing a good job at it." I scream in fright and whirl around with my hand over my heart, only to come face to face with the man who was just plaguing my thoughts.

"You scared the hell out of me!" I pant.

"There is too much in you to scare away." I shoot Derek a snotty look. Silence stretches between us for a moment until he breaks it. "The workers will be here shortly to open up, I want to show you something before they get here." My brows raise in surprise. When he turns and walks away, I chase after him. I don't know what he wants to show me but I'm just grateful he isn't being awkward about what he heard last night. I don't think I could take it if he brought it up.

When we round the back of the house, my brows furrow until I remember Cam said they had to move Hades back here.

"Are you taking me to him?" I ask with a note of excitement in my voice. Derek just lolls his head to the side and looks at me. He's looked at me hundreds of times before but not like this. I can see longing in his blue eyes and that shit steals the very oxygen I need from my lungs. I stumble but manage to catch myself before I fall. He stops a foot away from me, and the tension between us suddenly ramps up.

"Maddison—" Before he can say anything else, a white blur of movement catches my attention from the corner of my eye. I spin to the side to see Hades bounding toward the fence. I take off, ignoring Derek's plea for me to wait. I know they are all terrified of him, but I'm not. Hades would never hurt me because we are the same. We've been used, abandoned, and left with no family, and none of these were our choices. I head for the gate and try to pull it open at the same time Hades launches himself at the metal fence, but the gate doesn't budge.

I draw back when Hades begins to snarl and swipe at the fence, I stumble back a step only to smack into something. I look back over my shoulder to see it's Derek, his hands grip my waist instinctively.

"What happened to him?" I breathe out as I stare at my lion with heartbreak. He looks so angry and wild.

"He had his heart broken," he says in a tone laced with hurt, and I stiffen. "He has been out here alone since you left. No one has been able to get within a foot of his fence without him trying to tear them apart."

My heart sinks, guilt gnaws at me as I stare at my beautiful lion. I broke his heart and left him without a thought, like everyone else in his life—I chose my own self-preservation over him. I'm exactly like my mother, selfish.

"You are nothing like her, Maddison." The sound of his voice pulls me from my thoughts. The grip he has on my waist tightens possessively, drawing a gasp from me when he pulls me against his chest, eliminating the sliver of space between our bodies. Instantly my heart starts racing and my breathing turns ragged. It's only then that I realize I must have spoken my thoughts aloud. Shame washes over me.

"You have no idea, Derek. I am so much worse than her," I whisper.

"No, you're not," he argues.

I pull out of his hold and whirl around, facing him. I meet his intense gaze and refuse to cower under the shame of what happened the last time he and I were alone together.

"I may not fuck for money or put needles in my arm, but I am my mother's daughter. I left Hades. He was like a son to me and I didn't think twice before I ran." He opens his mouth to argue but I'm not done. "I know you heard us last night." His face instantly blanks, proving me right. "I may not ask for money like my mother would when she fucks three guys at once, but I sure as fuck want the three of you and I think you know that."

"I... sinner—"

"Save it, Derek. I know Cam was only saying what I wanted to hear, and believe me, I wish it was the truth but there is no way you would ever throw your morals out the window for your own stepdaughter. I get it, I really do, but no one truly knows who they are until they remove the mask they wear and take a long look at themselves in the mirror." I don't stick around for his reply, I head back to the house so I can change. They haven't asked me or even said anything about earning my keep but I still know how things are run, and I plan to pull my weight and work off the money I owe them for bailing me out.

I stand here long after she's gone and stare at the fucking lion that has been the bane of my existence for years.

"What would you do?" I ask Hades, knowing he won't answer.

"Yo, you coming?" I turn away from the beast and look up the path to see Royce and Cameron standing there. I release an agitated sigh and make my way toward them. We have a new act opening today and we have a lot to prepare before the first live circus show at ten this morning. We only run two shows a day, and are booked out solid for the next year. We are the only circus show in the US that doesn't go on the road. We have people traveling from all over the country to see us. We also own the local motel, campgrounds and one of the trailer parks. Those are all booked out for the next year as well.

I struggled being a single dad and learning how to take care of Cam with my brother. We were teenagers, kids having a kid really, but I knew I never wanted him to have the same life as me and struggle. I wanted more for him and that's why I started this carnival, which turned into a traveling circus over the years. Then when we got too busy and Cam needed somewhere to call home, we settled down and turned our land into our circus and carnival.

We spend the morning preparing everything for the first show. We're so under the gun and need this to go off without a hitch that we don't have two minutes to have a conversation. I'm annoyed because I wanted to speak with Cam about what was happening with him and Maddison. I don't exactly love the idea of him and Royce fucking but they are both adults and there isn't a lot I can say about it, plus I know Royce would never do anything to hurt my son or I would break his fucking jaw.

When I finally get a chance to sit down and take five minutes to myself, it's after nine at night and I still have a shit load of paperwork to get through. I'm behind on all of it and I keep putting it off because I hate the fucking hell out of using computers.

"I knew I'd find you in here." I flick my gaze up and watch Royce plonk his ass into the seat in front of my desk. I rest my elbows on the desk then bury my face in my hands, utterly exhausted and mentally drained. "I have never seen you this messed up over a girl before." I part my fingers and glare at him through the gaps, which just causes him to laugh.

"Fuck off and do some work, you prick," I snap.

"Oh, are you moping about our dirty little sinner?" I drop my hands and glare at Cameron, who is standing in the open doorway with a shit-eating grin on his face.

"Don't you have work to do as well?" I force out through clenched teeth. The little shit just stalks into my office and dumps a duffle bag I didn't see him holding onto my desk. I look from him to it then back again.

"You into some shady shit we don't know about?" Royce jokes. Cam shoots him a dry look then focuses back on me.

"You know when you have a touch screen phone you are more likely to pocket dial your son?" I frown at the idiot.

"What the hell are you talking about, Cameron?

I'm too busy and tired as hell for your shit tonight," I bite out.

"You pocket dialed me this morning. I heard everything Maddison said to you and I know just the way to help you, and both Royce and I, out with this situation."

My interest is captured and as much as I hate to admit it, I want to hear what he has to say. I'm four weeks away from being divorced from that bitch and getting her out of my life for good.

"Explain," I say as I recline back in my chair. Royce mimics my move but crosses his arms over his chest.

"Our little sinner has a primal kink and loves to be chased through the maze and fucked hard by a man in a mask." Cameron pulls three hoodies from the bag and dumps them on the desk only to reach back in, then holds up three masks. My jaw practically hits the fucking floor, they are disfigured clown masks that are terrifying and could be the star of your fucking nightmares. I reach out and grab one. They are thick plastic and lined with LED lights. This one has red diamonds over the eyes and a vicious smile, the mask an off white color. I don't miss the voice box inside to distort our voices.

I take in the other two Cameron holds, the three

of them are the same except for the color of the LED lights—the one in my hand has red lights, the two in his hands are blue and yellow lights. I notice the color of the diamonds on the eyes match the lighting.

"Put the mask on and be somebody else for the night. I know she has feelings for the three of us and it's because of that reason I never pushed her to label whatever we were. You aren't taking advantage of her, Dad. She wants you." I let Cameron's words wash over me. I understand his reasoning and I want to do as he says, but I am firm on the vows I took even if I hated the woman I was marrying.

I never consummated the marriage...

I latch onto that thought and run with it before I can change my mind and allow reason to creep in. I climb to my feet and don't miss the way both of those idiots grin at me.

"Where is she?" I ask, hearing the want in my own voice. Tonight I am going to hunt down the girl who has been plaguing my dreams since the moment I met her two years ago.

"Ferris wheel helping Carol," Cam answers. We waste no time pulling on the hoodies and masks. I go with the red one, Royce chooses the blue and Cam goes with the yellow. Some may think it's wrong that

I'm about to hunt down a woman with my son and fuck her senseless, but not us.

We are a different breed and share *everything*.

With a plan formulated, we waste no time as we all rush out of there and go in search of our prey. The three of us split up. I hide behind the doughnut stand and watch her. She looks fucking good enough to eat in her denim cut-offs and cropped black tee that shows off her toned stomach. I almost snort out loud when I read what her shirt says.

Snack.

"Thanks, Carol, but I can lock up," Maddison says.

"Thanks, sweetheart. I'll see you in the morning." Maddison waves her off, walks her to the gate, then locks it. When she makes her way over to the power box that will shut off all the lights, excitement rolls through me. The moment we are bathed in darkness I flick the switch on the mask to turn the LED lights on and dart out from behind the stand. The light from the moon casts enough light for me to see her wide-eyed reaction. She chokes on a scream and darts her gaze around us.

"Run, my dirty little sinner."

She turns and runs screaming for someone to help her. I chase her, eating up the space between us with ease. She is a foot in front of me as she runs around the corner, only to slam to a stop when she sees another masked man standing there. A scream tears from her at the sight of the yellow mask. Before she can veer left, I wrap my arm around her waist and lift her off the ground. She struggles in my hold but it's futile, I'm going to have her tonight and she is going to scream my name until her throat is hoarse and she's filled with my son's cock, while my brother is buried deep in her tight little ass.

<h2 style="text-align:center">SEVEN</h2>

MADDISON

"Help me!" I scream as I struggle against his hold. I kick my legs out as the yellow mask comes toward me. The guy behind me tosses me to him and he catches me with ease. He uses my moment of shock against me and turns me in his hold, so my back is to his chest. Red mask is on me in a second.

"Hold her arms." The robotic voice sends a shiver down my spine, I hate that I am terrified but also turned on. I get off on fear and it's fucking ridiculous considering the situation I'm currently in. Yellow mask obeys and traps my arms behind my back, easily overpowering me, rendering me powerless.

When red mask pops the button on my shorts, I whimper. "Please don't," I plead.

"Fear not, you will get a chance to escape, my dirty little toy," he says in that robotic voice as he pulls my shorts down my legs, leaving me in my black lace thong. When he skims his fingers along the small triangle of lace covering my pussy, I try to jerk away but he grips the lace and yellow mask holds me still. "I can't wait to taste this cunt."

"Fuck you!" I snarl. He pushes to his feet. I crane my neck back and refuse to look away as he tears my shirt open.

"Shit," he snaps when he realizes I'm not wearing a bra. I tense and bite down on my lip when he cups both my tits in his large hands.

"They're fucking perfect, aren't they?" yellow masks says behind me.

"I need to taste her," Red mask growls.

"I'll bite your fucking dick off before I ever let you fuck me," I hiss. I begin to tremble in fear when yellow mask pushes his face in the crook of my neck.

"You have five seconds to run. If we catch you, we're fucking you and I swear on my life you'll love it," he vows as he releases my arms. I shove red mask with all my might, then run as fast as I can, ignoring the sound of them counting behind me. I fly by the bumper cars and the pirate ship, hoping to find a place to hide. My phone was in the pocket of my shorts so I can't even call Cam or the others for help. The fastest way to Derek's office is through the horror maze, but the problem is they change the maze every night after we close. I'm about to head toward the circus tent only to skid to a stop when I spot another guy wearing a mask, but this one is blue. My eyes widen when I realize that there are three of them!

With no other choice, I head into the maze and pray I can make it out of here before they catch me. I loathe the fact that I am wet, my nipples pebbled and hard, begging for attention. My mind and body are at war with each other. I bite back a cry when I hear feet pounding the ground behind me. I hit a dead end and have to rush back the way I came and head right, I can see the lights of the blue mask and push my legs harder.

I take another wrong turn and growl in frustration as I run back and narrowly avoid being grabbed by the blue mask guy. I scream and push my legs even harder, praying that I can outrun him. When I see the opening of the maze exit I nearly cry out in joy, but the moment is over within a second when yellow mask steps into view, blocking my escape. I slide along the ground and lose my footing, falling face first onto the hard ground.

The wind rushes out of me. Before I have a chance to do anything, I'm grabbed and flipped onto my back. I throw my hands out and try to fight them off but yellow mask pins my wrists above my head while blue mask straddles me, using his weight to hold me in place.

"You are now off limits to everyone but *us*," Yellow mask declares.

"Fuck you, asshole, you don't own me," I scream.

"Oh, fuck, yes we do, baby," blue mask adds. I open my mouth to scream for Derek but when a red mask suddenly appears above me the words die on my tongue.

"Confess," he grits out. I jerk back and smack my head on the hard ground.

"I *confess* I am going to rip your cocks off," I hurl back at him.

"Hold her arms," he orders. Blue mask slips off me and is replaced by red mask, but instead of straddling my lap he pushes my legs open.

"I never got a taste before, but now I want to taste the whore who was screaming last night." His tone is laced with a hunger that not even the voice distorter can mask. A shiver runs down my spine and need courses throughout my body. But his words have me tensing, how the fuck do they know about last night?

"Taste the whore, brother," blue says. Red pushes his mask up to expose his mouth. Before I can fight or try and talk my way out of this, he buries his face in my pussy. I hate that my body reacts and a scream tears out of me when he swipes his tongue over my clit. I bite down on my lip to keep silent, cursing myself for enjoying the way his tongue pushes inside my tight hole.

"Don't be shy, he is going to be eating that dirty little cunt while we watch." I gasp and dart my gaze above me to see yellow watching. "I'll be watching every swipe of his tongue, listening to every sound you make as he strangles the fuck out of his cock while picturing his hand is your lips." I flick my gaze to blue and see yellow is right, he has his pants around his ankles and his cock in his hand. "*If* you're a good little slut, we might even choke you with your panties as I slide my cock inside your pussy and let one of them have your ass." His dirty promise has my breath hitching and my body taut with need. I've never fucked three guys at the same time but goddammit, now I want to. I'm so wet I can feel my arousal dripping out of me. I cry out in pleasure when he pushes two fingers inside me. I try to fight my body's reaction but I'm failing.

"Fucking dirty bitch," red mutters against my pussy.

"Punish the slut, she needs to be taught a lesson for teasing us," blue barks. My fear slowly bleeds away and is replaced with want. I should be disgusted with myself for allowing three strangers to do this to me but as my orgasm begins to build, I find myself not caring about the fact I don't know who they are. I picture each of them being Derek, Royce and Cam and fool myself into seeing their faces instead of the masks.

"You gonna bite my dick off if I put it in your mouth?" yellow asks. I shake my head. "Words," he snaps.

"No, I want to taste you," I admit, shocking not only him but myself.

"Get her on her hands and knees," yellow barks. I don't fight against them when they flip me over. Red instantly buries his face back into my pussy from behind, drawing a wanton scream from me. I watch as yellow pushes his sweats down and his cock springs free. The second my eyes lock onto the Prince Albert piercing, my jaw unhinges and my mouth waters. Cam has always wanted to get his cock pierced and I was all for it, because I wanted to know what it would feel like to taste metal in my mouth as I sucked his dick. Now I will get that chance. I just pray Derek, Royce or Cam don't come looking for me.

EIGHT
CAMERON

My mouth is watering from the sight of her cunt. It's the perfect color of pink, she was so wet and practically begging for Dad to eat her out. I lower to my knees in front of her, loving how her green eyes trail my every move. Dad and I have never done anything like this before together, but I'd be a liar if I said I wasn't excited to share this moment with him and Royce. She has never looked more stunning, on her knees panting and moaning.

Knowing that she can handle me and all my depraved wants and needs tells me she will be able to handle the three of us with ease. Royce and Dad are just as bad if not worse than me. When I fuck, I fuck hard and deep. I crave control. I reach out and trail my fingers along her luscious lips. She darts her tongue out and licks the tips of my fingers.

"Your eyes stay on me until I tell you otherwise, I don't give a fuck if he tells you to look at him, you obey *me*." Her eyes widen in shock. When Royce chuckles, I see she wants to look at him but she wisely heeds my warning and keeps her focus on me. I grip my cock and slowly ease it inside her waiting mouth. I groan at the feeling of having her lips wrapped around me again after so damn long.

"You like being a dirty little slut, don't you?" Royce grits out, I can hear the raw hunger lacing his words.

"Hmmm," she moans around my dick, the vibrations sending a shiver rolling down my spine. Her cheeks are red and her eyes are glazed with arousal. When she gags around my cock, I pull out, snap my arm out and grip her throat. Her eyes widen to the size of dinner plates. "I'm gonna come!"

Dad jerks back causing her to whimper. "You take what the fuck I give, you don't get to make demands. I say when you can come and how you come. Am I fucking clear, you little whore?" Her pupils dilate with need, her anxiety over my hold on her throat vanishes when Dad slips two fingers inside her cunt. "Answer me now!" he roars.

Her eyes roll back when he strokes that sweet spot inside her. "Yes. I'll take whatever you give me."

"I think she needs to be punished for speaking out of turn, don't you?" Royce says. I dart my gaze to him and smirk. The fucker has his cock in a death grip, it looks painful but I know he gets off on that shit.

Dad pulls out of her and shifts so he is flat on his back and pushes his pants down exposing his rock hard cock, I roll my eyes at the sight of his Jacob's ladder piercing. When he found out I got mine pierced, he had to one up me and get his done.

"Put that pussy on me now," he snaps. Maddison spins around and crawls up his legs until she is straddling his lap.

"Holy fuck," she breathes out when she grips his dick. I know that fucker would be smirking behind his mask.

"Put me inside you." She listens to him and rises up onto her knees, pushes her panties further to the side and lines his cock up with her entrance, before slowly lowering herself onto him,

"Holy shit, you're so big," she moans as she continues to ease onto him. Dad grips her waist and thrusts upward as he pulls her down onto him, sheathing himself fully inside her. They both cry out in ecstasy.

Not being able to control myself any longer, I push against her back until she is flush on his chest. My mouth waters, when I part her cheeks, at the sight of her puckered hole. Unable to stop myself I push my mask up and bury my face between her cheeks and force my tongue inside her ass so I can eat that booty like groceries. She screams but the sound is quickly muted when Royce grips her hair, yanks her head up and shoves his cock in her mouth, causing her to gag. To my surprise she pushes back against me. Most women get embarrassed about a man wanting to eat their ass, but not my sinner. The grubby little slut reaches back to grip my head to force me deeper as she grinds against my dad.

I smack her ass as I swirl my tongue around her puckered tight little hole. "Argh!" she cries out around Royce's dick. I draw back and spit. She growls her approval. I swirl the spit around her hole then reach into my pocket and grab the tube of lube I stashed in there and squirt it onto my dick.

I pull my mask down and line my cock up with her hole and slowly push forward. She tears free of Royce's dick and peers back at me over her shoulder. "I like it hard," she breathes out. When I grip the globes of her ass she stills and leans forward giving me better access. I pull back and squeeze the lube over her hole and begin swirling it around as she moans and wraps her lips around Royce again.

I am by no means small, I have both girth and length and I know how to use it as well. I am well versed in using my cock to its full capacity. Dad starts moving, distracting her while I continue fingering her ass, slowly stretching her to accommodate my size. She switches her mouth for her hand and yells. "Oh, shit. Please, please, please, let me come!" she cries out. Dad instantly stops moving and the sound of her growl has me smiling. I slowly ease my fingers from her and line my cock up with her ass again.

Her body stiffens and when she winces, I pull out and then slowly enter her again, making sure to take care so I don't hurt her. When I'm halfway in she sits up straight so her back is against my chest and forces me inside her further. She tilts her head back and beckons me with her eyes to claim her lips. I grant her wish and push my mask up enough to expose my mouth. When my tongue invades her mouth and I get a taste of her, I groan as I grip her waist in a bruising hold. She takes control and slowly begins to bounce up and down on us while never breaking the kiss or her hold on Royce's dick. Royce leans down and pinches her nipple. I swallow her cry and meet her next thrust with one of my own.

She breaks the kiss and screams out. "Shit. Fuck me like a whore, I've been a bad girl and I need to be punished." All three of us stare at her like she is a dream come true. Her eyes blaze with desire, as my own need rolls through me like a wave at her declaration. Royce wraps his hand around her throat, causing her to break the kiss and focus on him. The moment he has her focus he smacks her across the face. It's not hard and I've never been one who is into that type of thing but it's clear Maddison is. "Hit me again," she begs, he obeys.

Not wanting to be left out, I tug on her hair, forcing her head back so she can stare up at me. "Mouth open." I make sure to change my tone so she doesn't know it's me. She does as I demand. I hover over her mouth and then spit. She gasps but swallows. Her eyes are ablaze with lust and I just know she has found a new kink that she likes. "Open." She eagerly obeys me again but this time she moans when I spit in her mouth, and fuck me if that shit doesn't have my cock straining inside her.

"I need to come." She pants when we both thrust inside her tight holes.

I reach around and wrap my hand around her throat as Dad smacks both her tits. "Come on his cock, you dirty ass slut." My words are her undoing. She throws her head back and screams as her orgasm rips through her like an eruption. The sight of her dazed and shaking has my pace quickening, I need one more orgasm from her before I can come.

I'm on fire.

That orgasm was like nothing I have ever experienced before, I didn't have control over myself. I was at their mercy and I fucking loved every second of it. The sound of my screams still echo around the maze. I look down at red and my pussy quivers, just the sight of his cock buried deep inside me is almost better than any fucking fantasy I had about being fucked by the three guys I want most. But, when I peer over my shoulder and look at yellow, my stomach flutters and my mouth pops open as blue makes his way toward yellow and shoves his cock into his mouth.

I grow wetter just from the sight, thinking of how Cam sucked Royce's dick last night. The memory of how Royce ate my pussy while Cam thrust inside him savagely has my pussy clamping down on the cock inside me.

"You like watching him suck dick, baby?" red growls as he slams inside me, drawing a strangled moan from me.

"You love having both our cocks inside your dirty little holes don't you, while you watch him suck dick?" he adds.

I nod. "Yes. I love it but I need my mouth filled." They all groan but blue shoves his fingers in my mouth, shocking me. I gag.

"You only get our cocks, you greedy little slut," Red hisses as I feel another orgasm building. I was barely able to stay conscious after the first one.

It's too much.

Blue fucks my mouth with his fingers in sync with his thrusts into yellow's mouth. I lap at his two fingers and suck them hard. I envision his fingers being another cock and start riding them, taking control. To my surprise they allow it and let me take the lead. I set the pace, hard and fast. I feel both of their cocks swelling inside me, they're close. I hunger for the sight of them losing control and emptying everything they have inside me. I need to be filled with their cum, I want it coating every inch of my skin.

"You want our cum in you or on you?" red grits out. Blue withdraws his fingers so I can answer but not before he smears my spit all over my face and chest.

"I want it on me," I pant. Yellow reaches around my front and begins circling my clit. I shake my head trying to fight off the need to come. "I can't—"

When red's hand clamps over my mouth muting my reply. I tense. "Shut the fuck up and come like a good little slut." I sag against yellow, loving the dirty sinister words that come out of their mouths. Cam used to speak to me like this when we would fuck and that shit used to send me the hell over the edge. "Give me what I fucking want now so we can give you a triple facial." My eyes widen but I don't have a chance to process what he just said, because without warning my orgasm tears through me like an electric current. Red's hand mutes the sound of my screams. I have no time to come down before yellow is pulling out of me, then lifting me off red before he forces me to my knees.

"Hands behind your fucking back," blue snaps as the three of them stand in front of me with their dicks in their hands, their masks now firmly back in place. I do as I'm told, then moan at the sight of them jerking themselves. Aftershocks are still rolling through me and I clench my thighs together, trying to get a handle on myself but fail.

"Fuck, open your mouth," yellow roars a second before hot jets of his cum smack against my face. Some of it makes it onto my waiting tongue.

"Take it, you whore," blue snarls as he comes, his cum landing on my waiting tongue. Some of it makes it into my hair and onto my face. Both of them shudder and sag from the force of their release.

Red is the last to come, but when he does, he surprises me by shoving his cock into my open mouth. I keep my hands behind my back and force them to remain there as he tangles his hands in my hair and roars out his release. I choke on his cum but he still won't pull back, forcing me to swallow every last drop.

When he finally releases me and steps back, I almost slump forward but catch myself and suck in much needed air. When I finally look up, all their eyes are on me.

Blue surprises me when he crouches down, lifts his mask exposing his mouth, grips the back of my neck and forces me in close. He darts his tongue out then licks both of their cum off my face. Before I can grasp what he just did, he smashes his lips against mine and pushes his tongue inside my mouth. I suck on it, moaning at the strong taste of them. When he finally breaks our kiss, we are both breathless and gasping for air.

He pushes to his feet and pulls his pants up, the other two doing the same, while I remain on my knees watching their every move, still trying to process what just happened. When red and yellow turn to flee, blue looks down at me and says, "Same place tomorrow night, same time. But tomorrow, I'm fucking that pussy but I won't cum inside you, I'll cum in his ass while he fucks you and my other friend takes your ass."

My eyes widen as a new wave of need rolls through me. "I can't, my stepdad and stepbrother will notice I'm missing—"

"Don't worry, I'm sure they will be ever so understanding about our need to fuck you again," yellow adds with a cocky lilt to his voice.

"Don't make us wait. You won't like the punishment I dish out." His warning sends a thrill through me. I should be disgusted with myself but the truth is, I'm not, because living with Royce, Derek and Cam is going to have me on edge all hours of the day and night with no release. At least fucking these guys will ease some of that tension.

ROYCE

All I can think about is how good it felt to have her lips wrapped around my dick, it's been the only thought consuming me all day. I have a restless energy inside me as I watch the clock counting down the hours and willing the day away. Maddison was gone before we woke again and I know she is avoiding all of us. Part of me feels guilty for tricking her but that sinister side of me loves the fact she doesn't know it's us and is allowing her body the freedom to explore and embrace all our dark sides.

I told Cam and D this morning that I wanted to fuck her behind the grandstands during the last show. Both of them protested at first, but there is no chance of anyone seeing us while they are watching the show inside the tent, we just need to find a way to keep her quiet. The plan remains the same for tonight. My cock twitches with need as I think about watching Cam fuck her while my dick is deep in his ass and his father's cock inside her.

The three of us have had feelings for her for a long time. Cam and I don't fight ours but Derek fights his. I know he is stuck in his head about what happened last night and the only way for him to get over that is to get under her again tonight.

The guys and I have been holed up in Derek's office most of the day, trying to catch up on paperwork but not making a dent in it.

"Fuck this," Cam growls, then pulls his phone from his pocket and dials someone. Derek and I exchange a look. "Hey, can you meet me at Dad's office?" Derek's brows furrow and I shrug my shoulders. "Now. We need help with a job and you're the only one who can do it." When he ends the call he has a huge ass grin on his face.

"Who did you call?" I ask.

The little shit just wags his brows and shrugs. "Give it a minute." The room is bathed in silence as we wait. The second a knock sounds on the door, Cam's grin widens. "Come in." When the door opens, both Derek and I turn and to my utter surprise Maddison enters. She looks over at us and frowns, then turns back to Cam.

"What the fuck, Cameron?" she snaps.

He raises his hands as if surrendering. "I meant it. We really do need help and I know you are smart as hell and a fuck ton better at math than the three of us. Can you please help us with the accounts so we can sort our taxes?" This declaration surprises me, I had no idea she was a math whiz.

Maddy slowly turns to face me and Derek, takes a deep breath centering herself before she speaks, but the moment her eyes lock onto mine, all I can picture is her naked and riding Cam and D hard as she chased her own release.

"Can you show me the accounts?" Derek nods stiffly and motions for her to come over. She does as he asks and joins him behind the desk, then looks down at his computer screen, waiting. After a minute he starts cursing and blaming the stupid computer. She sighs and bats his hand off the mouse. Derek glares at the side of her head when she leans down and begins clicking a few buttons on the keyboard, then clicks the mouse a couple of times.

"You don't even have them set up in a spread-sheet for starters and you haven't followed any of the steps I taught you," she mutters, then shifts, forcing

Derek to roll back in his seat a bit. She hunches over further, giving D a perfect view of her ass. His blue eyes burn with want and when he grips the armrest of his chair in a punishing hold, I know it is taking everything inside him not to reach out and touch her.

"I'll get you a seat," Cam mutters but she just ignores him as she begins typing, then stops to shuffle through some of the papers until she finds the one she is looking for. Cam comes back a few minutes later and announces he has a seat for her but she doesn't look up or even acknowledge him as she sits down, but she doesn't sit in the right chair, instead she sits on Derek's lap. Her head snaps up as her eyes widen. Derek hisses and tenses beneath her. She leaps to her feet and whirls around facing Derek.

"I didn't mean to—"

"You're fine, sinner," he says. Upon hearing her nickname, she tenses and that's when it hits me. He called her that last night. Before she could hyper-focus on that I cut in to distract her train of thought.

"What can we do to help? Cam and I can file things while Derek continues sorting all the bookings on his laptop so you can have his desk." She fires off what she wants us to do in a flurry. The three of us all go about our tasks and keep out of her way. Unlike us, she seems to find a rhythm and manages to get through a lot of it before we call it quits at around seven. When we try to get Maddison to leave, she just waves us away, telling us she's nearly done so we leave her be.

The three of us finish feeding the animals in about an hour, then do a perimeter and ride check to make sure everything is powered down and locked up. Young kids tend to try and hide out, thinking they will be able to get the rides to work on their own. If that happens and one of them is hurt we'd lose everything, so we always make sure to do another check after the workers have all left. When we all arrive back at the house, none of the lights are on inside. Derek growls his annoyance. He's an impatient motherfucker and if she isn't waiting for us in the maze when we get there, Derek will make good on his warning and punish her pussy.

We walk back and stand in the same spot as last night, waiting for Maddison to show. Derek is having trouble keeping himself under control. Both Cam and I may be dominant but Derek is worse. Last night proved that. When he was the one calling the shots, it was almost natural for the both of us to submit to his control and follow his lead. I was surprised that I found it arousing being told what to do. I normally thrive on control and demand it from my sexual partners.

"Her pussy is about to weep," Derek snarls in that robotic tone a second before he spins on his heel and marches out of the maze. Both Cam and I chase after him, the only lighting is from our masks. Derek seems to have a bearing on where he is going so we follow without question. When his office building comes into view and we see no lights on or even a torch we come to a halt.

"Where the fuck is she?" Cam asks a second before we hear a squeal come from inside the circus tent. The three of us take off toward it. Before we enter, we pull our hoods up to cover our hair and step inside. The only lighting is from the small torch which is suspended in the air. I frown behind my mask as I wait for my eyes to adjust to the darkness and that's when I realize what I am seeing.

Maddison is stuck in the safety net for the trapeze.

You have got to be fucking kidding me!

Carol texted me to let me know they had forgotten to latch the trapeze. I'm terrified of heights and my dumb ass still agreed to help the old woman out because I'm an idiot. Everything was going fine until the lights shut off and I lost my footing and slipped off the landing. I swear to God my life flashed before my eyes as I fell. I knew the net was there but it didn't prevent the fear from engulfing me. Of course my stupid ass body is thrilled by the fear of almost dying and my pussy is aching for relief.

I take a moment to just lay here on the net and breathe as it slowly bounces me up and down. It's not that big of a jump from here to the ground so I'm not worried about being able to get down, until I spot a red light out of the corner of my eye and I realize now that I must be late. I roll over onto my stomach and stare wide eyed at the three masked guys from last night standing on the ground. All three of them are wearing the same black hoodies from last night and the masks conceal their identities.

A pang of longing hits me out of nowhere as I picture the three of them being Royce, Derek and Cameron.

"I warned you what would happen if you made me wait," red says as he takes a step forward. Instinctively I crawl backward on the net but he isn't having that. "You either get down here on your own or I come up there and drag your ass down by your hair... choose." Need curls inside me as his warning washes over me, slowly easing the fear from inside me as it's replaced by want.

I dart my gaze to the other two and watch as they both move in separate directions, surrounding me. I swallow audibly and weigh my options. Derek and the others went home ages ago, so I know they aren't near to hear me scream if these three tried anything so my only option is... I look around and when I spot my phone a couple feet away from me with the torch acting as a beacon, I snap my gaze back to red who seems to read my thoughts. We both move in unison.

I push to my feet just as he grips the edge of the net and heaves himself up, knocking me off balance. I scramble on my hands and knees toward my phone. I'm mere inches away from grabbing it when a hand locks around my ankle and drags me backward.

"Ahhhh," I cry out as I kick and try to sink my fingers through the holes in the net to halt my movement, but I can't. Red flips me onto my back. I expect him to pounce on me but to my horror he grips my hair and drags me forward by the strands, causing me cry out in pain as I feel some of my hair rip out. I'm on my hands and knees crawling after him toward the edge of the net. He manages to jump down gracefully but his grip on my hair never loosens as he pulls me over the edge.

I stumble and grunt from the force of hitting the ground but his hold on my hair keeps me from falling. I see the other two approaching us out of the corner of my eyes and growl my annoyance.

"Get your fucking hands off me!" I shout as I struggle in his hold, trying to get free. I clamp my mouth closed when he releases my hair only to grip my throat. I push up onto my tiptoes and claw at his arm as I struggle to breathe.

"My hands belong on you and you will never deny me the right to have you whenever and however the fuck I want. Am I clear?" I splutter and smack his arm, trying to loosen his hold. He squeezes tighter for a second before releasing me with a shove. I fall to my ass, gasping for air and rubbing my throat. The son of a bitch has no care for the pain he has just caused me as he moves forward until he is towering over me. "Get on your fucking knees... now!" I flick my gaze up to him and glare at the bastard.

I know he can see the malice in my eyes, the lighting of his mask would allow him a clear view. Yellow and blue come to flank him on either side, so I shoot them both the same look.

"Come on then, get your cocks out and try to put them in my mouth and see what I do," I threaten. When red crouches down in front of me and cocks his head to the side, I really do feel terror this time. Out of the three of them, it is easy to see he is the leader and the most unhinged.

When he places his hands on the tops of my shins I turn to stone. My eyes remain locked on him as he slowly trails them up my legs until he reaches my thighs and digs his fingers into my soft flesh, causing me to wince. He pushes forward until the rough plastic of his horrific mask is pressed against my face. I look deep into his eyes and fight the frustration of not being able to see the color of them with him being this close. These masks plagued my night-mares last night.

"I love it when they play rough," he says in a creepy robotic tone. "It makes breaking them and bending them to my will all that much sweeter." I recoil. "You coming on my cock last night proves you are a filthy little liar. We're going to make you so dirty and rotten to the fucking core that you will be ruined for any other man."

His words may have me itching with need but the fighter in me refuses to go down without a fight. "I know three men who have already ruined me for anyone else, so do your worst." His grip on my legs tightens. I bite down on the inside of my cheek to keep from crying out. The sand from the arena is biting into the back of my legs but I refuse to show him my discomfort.

"Tonight, we're going to do things to you that will blow your wildest dreams out of the fucking water," Yellow says, drawing my focus to him. Red releases me and pushes to his feet. I watch as he reaches behind himself and pulls out a...

"You have a fucking crop?" I hiss and scurry backward along the sand, ignoring the sting as it bites into my flesh.

"Hold her," red barks. Before I can get to my

feet, yellow and blue grab and hold me down on my back, with a knee on each of my arms.

"Fuck you!" I scream when red makes his way toward us. I kick and scream when he reaches down and begins undoing my pants. "Derek!" I scream. I'm into some fucked up shit sexually but I have never been whipped. "Royce!" I call out praying they are trying to find me. "Cameron!" I startle when yellow cups my cheek so softly. Before I can focus too much on him, red yanks my pants down my legs, leaving me in nothing but my thong, again.

"Who did you wear this for?" the bastard has the nerve to ask. I glare at the motherfucker.

"I wore red tonight in the hopes my stepbrother and stepdaddy would take turns on me." Blue chuckles, earning a scowl from me. Red doesn't bother using words, the bastard just jerks his arm back that is holding the crop and smacks my pussy. I cry out and thrash in the other two's hold, hurling threats at each of them as red smacks my pussy again and this time, I'm mortified to realize I actually like it.

"Can your daddy make you feel as good as we do?" blue asks as red smacks the inside of my thighs when I close my legs. When I still refuse to open them, he smacks them again, but this time there is a bite to the whip and I scream.

"Show me my pussy, Maddison." I still at the sound of my name coming from red. I slowly open my legs, not wanting him to hurt me again.

"Answer me, bitch," blue snarls. I peer up at him as red swirls the crop against my lace covered pussy, forcing a shiver of desire from me.

"Daddy can make me speak in tongues," I taunt, then turn and look up at yellow as I say, "You should see how my brother fucks me, *hmmm*," I moan. "The way Cam can make me come so hard and forget my own name is a skill none of you will ever master." My declaration renders them all silent and still. Victory courses through me and I smirk at red triumphantly.

He wipes the smile off my face with his next words. "Challenge accepted, sinner," red vows.

TWELVE

DEREK

I drop to my knees before her and push her panties to the side, exposing her perfect pink pussy that is glistening with her arousal. She talks a big game but the girl is full of shit. She's getting off on us treating her like a little fuck doll.

The urge to tear my mask off and reveal who I am is strong. I want to show her my face as I slide my cock inside her and watch as her eyes round with surprise, before I wipe the look from her beautiful face and replace it with hunger.

"Your ass is mine tonight," I growl as I glide a finger through her slick folds. She cries out and arches her back as much as she can. When I push that finger inside her tight, wet little hole, she begins to tremble just from my touch. I hook my finger at the right angle and rub against that sweet spot inside her. Cameron pulls her shirt up to expose a matching red bra. I hum my approval at the sight but the instant he and Royce yank the cups down, exposing her mouth-watering tits, I groan. They pinch her nipples hard and she screams in pleasure.

"You gonna take our cocks like a good little whore, baby?" Cam asks as I insert a second finger, loving the sounds she makes.

"Fuck, yes, I'll take all three of you." She pants.

"Nuh-uh. Tonight my brother gets your ass while I get your pussy but don't worry, you get to watch my yellow friend here fuck me as I take you over the edge." Her breath hitches at Royce's vow. She flicks her eyes to me and I see pure unfiltered hunger shining in the depths of those green eyes. My cock is so hard for her it's actually painful, I need to be inside her within the next minute or I'm gonna fucking explode. As if they can read my thoughts, both of the guys shift and release her. Maddison tentatively sits up and looks between the three of us but when her gaze finally settles on me, I smirk.

I watch the transformation as she tugs her shirt the remainder of the way off, then slowly stands, leaving Cam and Royce on their knees either side of her. Both of them reach out and trail their hands up her naked legs. She reaches behind her back and unsnaps her bra, letting the straps slide down her arms before it drops to the ground. She doesn't fight when Cam reaches up and slowly peels her thong down her legs. She steps forward and crouches down to retrieve her ruined thong from the ground, then swaggers toward me with the grace of a wet dream.

She comes to a stop an inch away. I fight to keep my hands at my sides and not reach out and grab her. She lifts her hand holding the scrap of her lace thong pinched between her fingers. I remain silent, waiting to see what she will do next. A devilish glint enters her eyes as she slowly lowers to her knees before me. She keeps her eyes on me as she stuffs her panties in my pocket, then proceeds to begin undoing my pants. Cam and Royce both scramble over to us when she frees my cock. She pays them no mind as she grips my cock, pulling a hiss from me.

Her eyes remain locked on mine as she darts her tongue out and licks my Jacob's ladder. I throw my head back and groan when she wraps her lips around my dick. I get lost in the feeling of her hot mouth wrapped around me until I hear Cam and Royce both groan. My head lolls forward to see her bobbing up and down on my dick while she jerks them off. She switches between the three of us sucking and stroking each of us, making sure to drive us all fucking insane with need.

"Fuck." I tear my dick out of her hand and ignore the other two growls of annoyance when I grip her hair and tug her free of Cam's dick and drag her with me toward the grandstands. I release her and take a seat, the bite of the cool metal does nothing to ease the inferno burning inside me. She stands there staring down at me with lust filled eyes.

"Here," Royce says, then tosses me a tube. I'm surprised I caught it with no light in here aside from our masks and her torch. Before I can do anything with the lube she snatches it from my hand and pops the top, squirts some into her hand then massages it onto my cock. Curses tumble from my lips at the feeling of her hand on me again. I reach for the lube when she releases my dick but she holds it out of reach and squirts more onto her hand then tosses the tube to the side as she turns and bends at the waist.

"Part my ass for me," she purrs. Without over thinking it I do as she says, and watch with hunger as she reaches back and begins circling her tight hole. Cam and Royce both move in closer and watch her, each of them with their dicks in their hands. "Oh God," she moans when she pushes a finger inside her ass. Unable to control myself any longer, I yank her hand free, then grip her waist and pull back.

"Lower that ass onto my cock, then lift your legs so my brother can fuck that pussy." She moans softly and begins to slowly lower herself onto my waiting dick. I expect her to take a few minutes to adjust and get used to my size but the moment I breach her tight hole, she continues to lower herself onto me without needing a break.

"Jesus, fuck, yes. You feel so good," she cries out as she slams down onto me, drawing a roar of plea-sure from me. It takes me a minute to control myself. She leans back against my chest and lifts her legs, forcing me to recline as far as I can, until my back is pressed against the seat behind us. I grip her legs behind her knees and hold them wide as Royce moves in front of her. He lines his cock up with her entrance and slams inside her, causing her to bow off my chest and scream out.

"Fuck, you're so tight, baby," Royce growls. Cam slides in behind Royce and pushes him forward until he is pressed against Maddison. The three of us remain still as we hear him squirting lube onto his hand. Maddison keeps her gaze focused over Royce's shoulder and watches with rapt attention as my son slowly pushes inside my best friend. When Cameron thrusts inside him we groan from the movement. "You like that, baby?"

Maddy nods her head. "It's the hottest fucking thing I have ever seen," she breathes out a second before Cam thrusts his hips, causing Royce to move inside her. It takes us a beat for us to find a rhythm but when we do it is fucking euphoric. I meet Cam and Royce thrust for thrust. Maddy locks one arm around Royce's neck and the other around mine and starts trying to bounce up and down on our dicks causing the both of us to curse.

"Like that, please don't stop," she bellows. I reach around her and twirl her nipples between my fingers.

"I'm close. I'm gonna fill this ass up with my cum," Cam grits out through clenched teeth.

"Fuck me harder, I want to cum with you," Royce yells.

"Oh fuck, yes, yes, yes!" Maddison screams as her orgasm tears through her like a herd of wild horses. Her screams fill the massive tent and a wave of possessiveness washes over me. No one else will ever get to see her or hear her come, I vow it. She may not realize it but this girl now belongs to the three of us and we will never fucking let her go. When she finds out it's us behind the masks, she better accept it. Because, if she tries to run, this time I will chase her ass down and drag her back here by her fucking hair—this pussy is ours.

This dirty little sinner is owned by us.

"I'm coming," Cam roars. I thrust inside her harder, chasing my own release as Royce follows behind Cam seconds later. They both pull out and leave me with her on my own. I push to my feet as she tips her head back to stare up at me with a dazed look in her eyes. Using the grip I have on her legs, I lift her up and down on my cock, loving the screams of pleasure coming from her.

"I need you to get there and come with me, baby," I force out through clenched teeth.

She shakes her head. "I can't," she cries out. Before I can snarl at her to give me what I want, Cam drops to his knees and lifts his mask to expose his mouth, then begins eating her pussy. She arches forward and screams so fucking loud I swear Hades would be able to hear her.

"You like his mouth on your cunt, you nasty little slut?" Royce purrs from behind Cam.

"Yes, I fucking love it," she breathes out as a single shudder rolls through her.

"I need you to come!" I snap as I thrust inside her. We both lose control in unison. I shatter and empty everything I have inside her tight little hole, her name like a prayer from my lips as I yell it to the gods above. Tremors continue to roll through me unchecked and her breaths are coming in short, ragged pants as she comes down from her climax.

"Hold her still," Cam barks. I peer down over her shoulder and watch as he sucks on her pussy, pulling another loud cry from her. He pulls back and climbs to his feet, grips her chin and forces her mouth open, then spits Royce's cum into her mouth. "Swallow." She obeys without complaint.

She is the dirtiest bitch I have ever met and I fucking love it.

It's been nearly two weeks since I arrived back here with Cam. Every night I meet up with the masked clowns and allow them to do unspeakable things to me. Last night, red tried to force me to swallow every drop of his cum.

When he pulled back, I spat it on the ground by his feet. Blue smacked me across the face and shoved his cock down my throat. I made sure to swallow every last drop of his release, which caused red to promise to punish me tonight.

I love how violent blue gets when we fuck. Yellow is the more tentative one but he's just as fucking nasty. He loves cum swapping and spitting in my mouth or on me. Red, on the other hand, is unhinged and vulgar. He doesn't ask for permission, he just takes what he wants and forces me to take everything he gives me.

I clench my thighs together and bite down on my lip to keep from moaning out loud as I picture how they made me come so many times last night I passed out, only to wake up in my bed this morning with no idea how the fuck I got back to the house.

"You're looking a bit flushed, sinner." I snap my head toward Cam and narrow my eyes. The fucker just grins at me from his place behind his desk. Every day I have been holed up in Derek's office with them, helping to fix the accounts. I still leave the house before they wake and go down to see Hades . He doesn't seem as angry anymore but Derek still refuses to give me the keys to his pen.

"Leave her alone," Derek snaps, earning an eye roll from his son. "Maddy?" I flick my gaze to him and fight not to squirm under the pressure of it. "You have your court date next week." My mood instantly sours, I can feel Cam and Royce staring at me but I keep my focus on Derek as I answer.

"Given this is the fourth time I've been arrested because of her, I don't like my chances of getting off," I admit bitterly.

"How the fuck can she get away with this?" Cam

voices aloud. I slump back in my chair behind Derek's desk and sigh.

"She's Joanne Leigh. She's like a fucking cockroach and can crawl her way out of any situation, or fuck her way out." I wince when I realize what I just said and shoot Derek an apologetic look. He waves away my concern.

"Short of finding her and making her confess, what are our options?" Royce asks Derek. To his credit Derek tries not to look disheartened, we all know my chances of not going prison are slim. Bitterness fills me, I know without a doubt that Joanne won't come to my rescue and save me.

"There is nothing any of you can do. I'm grateful you all let me stay while I tried to figure out what to do, but it's pointless," I say with defeat thick in my tone.

"Fuck that!" Cam snaps and stands from his seat, looking at his father. "I'm not letting her go." His declaration has me reeling back and mouth parting on a silent gasp.

"She isn't going anywhere, Son. We'll figure this out," Derek says with such conviction I actually believe him.

"This is her home and I'll be damned if I let the likes of her trashy mother take that from her," Royce adds. My heart swells and for the first time in a long time, I actually feel like I belong. God, what I wouldn't give to call the three of them mine. I shouldn't want the man who is still married to my mother but I can't help it. Cam has told me none of them have spoken to my mother since she fled in the middle of the night and left me behind.

I bury myself in work for the rest of the day, trying to keep my mind busy. When Cam tells us it's after five, I decide to leave early and go see Hades before I shower and go meet my masked men. Tonight they told me to meet them in carnival row. That's the lane where all our games are played. I have no idea what to expect but I'm excited to find out. When Hades sees me approaching, he makes his way slowly toward the fence. When he brushes up against the steel I brush my fingers along it feeling wisps of his fur. Longing slams into me, I don't want to leave him or this place again.

"I might have to go away again," I say quietly. Hades continues to brush against the fence without a care in the world. "This time it won't be by choice. I should never have left you the first time," I admit. "I swear, I won't give up and I'll make sure I am always here for you, boy. It's gonna be me and you against the world," I promise.

I take my time getting dressed. It's starting to get cooler now and in a couple of months the Vought Jacob's Carnival will close down for winter. I choose to go with a dress tonight and pair it with a cream cardigan and my low cut chucks. I tie my hair in a high ponytail and apply some lip gloss before deeming myself ready. I have no idea where the guys are, so I check to make sure the hallway is clear before quietly exiting and pulling my door softly closed behind me.

All the lights are out in the house. I slowly creep down the stairs and head for the door, but freeze at the sound of his voice behind me.

"Going somewhere, sinner?" I scrunch my eyes closed and keep my back to Derek as I answer.

"Just going to check on…" I wrack my brain for any excuse but come up blank, so I decide to push my luck and see if I can crack Derek's armor. "I'm meeting someone."

"Hmmm." I peer over my shoulder at him and can just make out his silhouette in the darkness.

"What's that supposed to mean?"

Derek steps in closer to me and my breath hitches. In a bold move I never saw coming, he grabs my waist and spins me around to face him, using his body to push me back against the closed door. His free hand lands with a hard thud above my head. My chest is rising and falling so fast that I can't take a deep breath. My blood is roaring in my ears, I whimper when he bends down and I feel his lips brush against the shell of my ear, sending a delicious shiver down my spine and liquid pooling between my thighs.

"It means you shouldn't have to sneak out to get *fucked*." I gasp loudly. The hand that grips my waist trails down my side, then he pushes it under my dress and cups my pussy, drawing a loud moan from me. His finger grazes my throbbing cunt as he speaks. "When you realize what you've had all along, you'll stop playing coy and understand you were always *mine* from the moment I laid eyes on you." Before I can process what the fuck he just said, he bites down on my earlobe, then jerks away from me and disappears into the darkness.

My knees grow weak and my breathing is erratic as hell as I stand here, trying to get control over my body and will my pussy to stop pulsing with need.

God, I thought I wanted him bad before, but I was wrong. I *need* Daddy to make me scream his name and one day, I will make that dream a reality. Until then, I have three masked men to meet so they can rid me of this ache he caused.

FOURTEEN

CAMERON

By the time she arrives, the three of us are ready and waiting. The second she spots us standing in the middle of carnival row with our masks as the only source of lighting. Excitement thrums through me at the thought of what we will do to her tonight. I take in her outfit and gnaw on my bottom lip as a surge of desire rolls through me. Maddy isn't the type of girl who wears dresses and I have only ever seen her wear one once before. Knowing she wore this for the three of us has me wanting to pound my fist against my chest like a fucking caveman.

Royce breaks away from the three of us and saunters toward her with a swagger only he could pull off. Maddy remains still as he approaches. I want to growl in frustration when she pulls her beautiful eyes from us to focus on him. I watch with hunger as Royce reaches out and grips the back of her neck, yanking her against him. She splays her hands on his chest and peers up at him.

"Tonight, you are to be punished by my brother for wasting the gift he gave you last night," Royce announces. Maddy is a fucking temptress and proves me right when she turns her head as much as Royce's hold allows and looks directly at my dad.

"Do your worst, red," she purrs in a seductive tone that has my dick twitching in my pants.

A dark robotic laugh comes from my dad as he crosses his arms over his chest. "Get on your hands and knees and crawl to me." Maddy's eyes widen a second before she looks back to Royce. I shake my head. If she thinks for one second he will help her out she is out of her mind. Royce gets off on this type of shit, we all do. He releases her and steps back, then sweeps his arm out toward us. Our dirty little sinner looks between the three of us, hoping one of us will save her from this but she's on her own with this one.

Her nostrils flare in outrage. I expect her to fight and refuse, forcing us to make her obey, but then she shucks off her cardigan and tosses it at Royce, who catches it by instinct, then slowly lowers to her knees. When she begins to crawl toward him, I'm suddenly grateful for my mask to cover the shocked expression on my face. Maddy's eyes are twin flames as she scowls at my dad. All he does is widen his stance and keeps his focus on her. The closer she gets, the harder my dick becomes. I've had fantasies about her crawling toward me exactly like this and seeing that dream come true is fucking euphoric.

When she is mere feet from us, Dad speaks. "Stop." She freezes on the spot and looks up at him with fire swirling in those eyes. "Tonight you don't have the privilege of seeing who is doing what, you just get to *feel*." Her brows furrow in confusion until Royce steps behind her and secures a blindfold around her eyes. Once it's secured she sits back on her haunches. "You'll be bound, gagged and utterly at our mercy." A tremble runs through her. I step forward and grab one of her arms while Royce grabs the other and we haul her to her feet.

We lead her toward the wheel of death. Her breathing turns shallow when we spin her around and begin securing her wrists and ankles with the straps. I can feel the panic wafting off her in waves. We have pushed her boundaries and forced her to her limits each night but she has never been blind-folded and restrained.

I remove my mask and lean in, allowing my stubble to scrape against her cheek. She gasps in surprise. I force my voice deeper to mask my tone as I say, "You can say *stop* at any time." My reassurance seems to put some of her worries at ease and she relaxes in her restraints. Unable to control the urge, I capture her lips in a kiss filled with longing and want. I wish more than anything I could rip this blindfold off her and show her that it's us, but I know Dad isn't ready for that step yet. She opens for me without a fight. I brush my tongue against hers and relish the sound she makes when she gets to taste me.

I run my hands along her side, loving the way she trembles from my touch. Without breaking the kiss, I begin to pop the buttons on the front of her dress, breaking the kiss when I get about halfway. A smile stretches across my face when she whimpers at the loss of my mouth. Royce grips her chin as I drop to my knees before her, then he claims her lips. I whistle when I push the dress open and take in what she is wearing—a deep green bralette with matching panties. Dad groans behind me, green is his favorite color.

Royce gropes her tits as I reach out and push her

panties to the side and growl my approval at how fucking wet she is. "Good girl," I praise before swiping my tongue through her slit. She's so turned on I know she won't last long. Royce swallows her cries of bliss as I eat her dripping cunt, loving how her juices begin to leak down my chin and mark me as hers. I love having the smell of her pussy on me so I can jerk off to her scent later or better yet, force Royce to blow me while I think about her.

"They're making you feel so good, aren't they?" Dad asks in that robotic voice, still wearing his mask.

"Hmmmm," she murmurs while continuing to kiss Royce.

"I bet you want to come, don't you, our filthy little whore?" She groans in response to his question. "But you denied me the pleasure of seeing you swallow my cum, so tonight you will beg." She stiffens as his words slowly sink in. "Enough." Both Royce and I pull back.

"No!" she cries out and tugs against her restraints.

"You were warned that you would be punished tonight. I should leave you tied here like a wanton slut so everyone can see how much of a whore you are in the morning." His words don't fill her with fear, if anything they just serve to heighten her arousal. "You'd like them seeing you get fucked by us, wouldn't you?" She opens her mouth to answer but then snaps it closed, as if thinking better about baiting him. "You're learning," he praises, then waves his hand for Royce and me to go back to eating her out and playing with her tits. This time Royce doesn't kiss her, but yanks the cups of her bra down and begins sucking on her nipples. When she's about to come, we pull back. Maddison screams in frustration.

Orgasm denial is one of the best forms of torture.

"You want to come?" Dad asks again.

She nods furiously. "Yes, please, please, please, let me come!" she screams. Royce and I look back at him. When he nods we resume our roles and continue driving her out of her mind. This time I slide two fingers inside her tight little hole, loving the sound of the scream that rips free from her when I stroke that spot inside her that has her speaking in tongues. The moment I feel her pussy walls clamping down on my fingers, I pull free of her and push to my feet. This time when she screams in frustration, tears leak down her cheeks. The sight of them has a growl rumbling from me. I lean forward and lick them away.

"Time to pay for your crime," Royce says in a

tone I don't recognize. Dad pushes past us and spins the wheel so she is upside down. She squeals in surprise, her pussy now eye level with him. He tears his mask off and tosses it to the side a second before he buries face inside her cunt and feasts on her like a savage devouring his last meal.

Everything is so sensitive. The blood is rushing to my head but I'm so tight with tension from being denied my orgasms. The feeling of his mouth on my pussy is fucking electric. I won't survive being denied again. I swear to God I need this climax more than I need my next damn breath.

"Oh, fuck yes. Please, please don't stop. I'll do whatever you want just let me fucking come!" I scream out as he pushes his tongue inside my pussy. The blood is pounding in my ears and the head rush I'm getting is only serving to make everything feel ten times more intense. Every stroke of his tongue sends a current through me like a live wire shocking me from a slumber. I can feel my climax breaching the horizon and I try to latch onto it with everything

I have but it's like he knows and laughs darkly. "Please, I swear I won't disobey you!" Fuck, I would promise to tongue his asshole right now if he just lets me come.

To my utter relief he doesn't stop. The orgasm tears through me like a tsunami. I forget how to breathe for a moment until a scream so primal tears out of me, then to my utter horror I feel myself squirt.

I have never done that before.

Before I can process what the fuck just happened or deal with the fact I can feel myself still squirting, I'm spun again until I'm upright. A hand closes around my throat.

"You've been holding out on us," one of them growls.

I shake my head. "I've never—" My reply is cut off when someone smacks my pussy, sparking another orgasm. I'm unprepared for it and it robs me of oxygen as it bursts through me with a blazing heat making me feel like my body is on fire. My mortification continues when he smacks me again, making me squirt. My jaw unhinges when I hear someone slurping. I have no time to process the fact that someone is drinking my cum when a hand grips my chin and forces my mouth open, then spits something into my mouth. I swallow instinctively only to realize that it was my own release I just tasted and fuck, it tastes so good.

"The dirty little slut likes it." His voice is so deep and gravelly it sends a shiver down my spine. After-shocks still roll through me—having two orgasms back to back like that has taken it out of me, especially that first one. That was *the* most intense climax I have ever experienced.

"Awww, don't get sleepy on us now, baby. We're not done with you." Normally hearing that would thrill me but tonight, I'm just fucking worried that another orgasm will cause me to black out and with these three, that is definitely on the cards because they are so far from selfish when it comes to making sure I am taken care of it's not funny.

I shake my head. "I can't," I plead.

"You can and you fucking will," one of them snarls in a robotic voice that I am used to as another pushes two fingers inside my quivering pussy, drawing a heady moan from me. "Give me what I want," he demands. I try to tug on my restraints, but it's futile. There is no breaking free of these leather straps, they hold Luther's weight as Connie hurls knives at him. My back arches forward as a wave of pleasure rolls through me with the force of a rip tide.

I know I'm seconds away from coming and there isn't a thing I can do to stop it. "Come for me, sinner," are the last words I hear before my orgasm erupts and tears me in half, pulling a roar so loud from me that even Hades would be proud. But the pleasure is too much and I black out.

I wake to the feeling of being jostled. I keep my eyes closed as I realize I'm being carried and tucked against one of their chests. The warmth seeping into me from how close he is soothes me. These three masked strangers are making me feel things I never thought I would ever get the chance to experience in my life.

I'm so confused.

My feelings for Royce, Derek and Cameron haven't lessened. Even being away from them for a year the feelings remained. Allowing these three to ravage my body and push me to the limits each night as I explore all my sexual desires still hasn't dimmed my desire toward the three of them. Every morning I wake, a pang hits me and I feel regret over fucking red, yellow and blue. I wish more than anything that it was the others meeting me every night and bringing my wild fantasies to life.

Realization hits me, this will be over soon and I won't get a chance to meet with these three anymore and my hope of Derek, Cam and Royce ever returning my feelings will be nothing but a pipe dream. I'll be locked up for years all because my mom is a piece of shit.

"Take her to her room." At the sound of the robotic voice coming from my left I tense, unintentionally alerting the one carrying me that I'm awake. We pause mid step and I slowly open my eyes, knowing there is no point faking sleep when he knows I'm awake. I look up and am met with the blaring lights from blue's mask. The moon is full and bright tonight giving me a view of his eyes. They're a rich brown and hold a warmth that I never expected to see considering how he fucks.

Their masks scared the hell out of me at the beginning—the sinister smile that sent a shiver down my spine, the way the white of the mask looks like skin peeling and the diamonds around the eyes that just add an ominous look to them. But the lights, they only served to enhance the horror of what you were seeing, giving you a clear view of your worst nightmare brought to life. But now, all I see is the three men who spend their nights ensuring I receive the greatest pleasure and allow me to explore my wants without judgment. I may not know who they are and know nothing about them aside from how they make me feel, but we've built a trust of sorts.

I allow them control and they offer me security.

"Who are you?" I blurt out. I search his eyes trying to find a single tell. Those brown eyes make me feel safe like... I'm home. They seem so familiar but I don't delude myself into thinking I know who he is.

"Your past colliding with your present." Blue's answer has my brows bunching. He slowly lowers me to my feet, only stepping back when he's sure I'm able to stand on my own. I peer down at my clothes and a warmth spreads through me when I see they have buttoned my dress and even tied my cardigan around my waist. I look up as yellow and red flank blue. I run my gaze over each of them and need coils inside me until I realize where we are. I spin around and gasp at the sight of the house.

"Time is ticking, Maddison. When faced with the choice of continuing to live in sin, will you accept it or will you repent?" I look back at red and cock my head to the side, mulling over his words.

"I'm not religious," I say.

Yellow answers for him, drawing my attention to him. "You need to go to church to believe in a higher power. Choosing this means judgment and living in sin. Is that an option or a hard limit?" I don't get to process his words or even formulate a response before the three of them turn their backs to me and stalk off into the darkness, with their masks as the only source of lighting.

SIXTEEN

ROYCE

The tension in the office this morning is thick enough to choke the fucking life out of you. Derek has been on edge since last night after we left Maddy. I've tried to ask him what's up but he is being tight lipped. Cam is lost in his head and I know he wants to tell her the truth but Derek won't let him. He's worried about something and I have no idea what the fuck it is. This is the first time me and my brother have not been on the same page about something. I can usually read him like an open book but he is purposefully shielding himself off, and that shit is concerning. The only time he has ever done something like this was when he married Joanne.

I look over at our dirty little sinner and marvel at how fucking gorgeous she is. Every single time she walks into a room, she steals the air from my lungs and my fucking heart constricts. The organ now only beats for her. It is hers to command and control. I've never fallen in love or even wanted something more than a woman to warm my bed for a night but with Maddison, I don't want this to end.

"I should have all of these accounts in order before I... leave." The sound of her voice pulls me from my thoughts.

"You aren't going anywhere," Cameron says with conviction. Maddy shoots him a sad smile which just infuriates me.

"Don't fucking look like that," I snap. She swings her gaze to me, surprise written all over her face at my tone. "You aren't going to prison, your ass is staying right fucking here where it belongs." My declaration has her mouth parting in stupor. I feel the same way Cameron does, I want her to know it's us. Her asking who we were last night nearly had me dropping to my knees and begging her to understand that we only wore the masks so we could have the chance to finally touch her and fool ourselves into thinking she could be ours for a short amount of time. The age gap between her and I is huge. She's so young and has a lot of life to live and could find someone her own age to experience things with, but

I'm a selfish motherfucker and refuse to allow anyone else to touch her.

"Royce," she says my name like it's a fucking prayer, and I have to bite back my groan. "My mother will never show up and confess that she lied. The cops never believed me when I told them and the judge sure as fuck won't either. I am so grateful the three of you have my back, but I'm also not an idiot. I'm going to jail and no matter how many times you guys try to convince me I won't—"

"Shut the fuck up!" Derek roars. Maddison recoils in her seat behind his desk. Cam and I both snap our gazes to him in shock. He stands there with his fists clenched at his sides, anger seeping from his pores as he stares at her. "You won't go to prison because I made sure of that." His tone is calm and even but it's filled with warning.

Maddison darts her eyes around the room, trying to gauge if Cam and I know what he is talking about but we are just as stumped as she is. "What do you mean?" she asks quietly.

Derek's reply is curt and filled with hatred. "She'll be here tonight."

Maddy's face drops. She slowly pushes to her feet and stares at Derek with betrayal in her eyes. "Joanne is coming here?" Her tone is void of emotion, the broken look flashing in her eyes has my stomach bottoming out and the need to break my brother's jaw rushes through me. When he nods, Cam and I both suck in a sharp breath. He told us that he had no contact with her after she left. A sense of betrayal washes over me, Derek has never kept anything from me, we're partners in everything.

"She will make a statement and free you from these charges—" Maddison holds a hand up, silencing Derek. I can see her battling back tears as she stares at him, and it's taking everything inside me not to go to her, wrap her in my arms to offer her my support. Cam looks like he wants to tear his father to shreds and I'll admit, I wouldn't stop him. I want to tear my pound of flesh from him as well for hurting Maddy.

"You lied to me." Her quietly spoken words shred me, her tone laced with pain. Derek opens his mouth to defend himself but she pushes on. "I trusted you, Derek!" She may have said the words barely above a whisper but the force behind them has him stumbling back a step. Maddison doesn't stay put, she rushes out of the office with Cameron hot on her heels. I shoot Derek a look that promises pain if he has fucked this up for us before shouldering past him, following after Cam and Maddison.

I follow the sound of Cam's voice, calling for Maddy to stop. I'm running after them, trying to catch her before she can get too far. We need a chance to explain to her that we had nothing to do with this and that Derek acted alone. My anger toward my brother only grows the longer she refuses to stop. When she passes the house, a frown pulls at my brows until I finally understand where she is going. I push my legs harder, trying to gain on her. If she reaches her destination we will never be able to get near her and he will make sure of that!

"Cam, tackle her if you have to!" I roar. He wastes time peering over his shoulder at me, giving a couple more seconds of leeway and that time costs us. We're too late. She begins scaling the fence and there isn't a damn thing we can do to stop her.

"Hades!" she screams her lion's name, so loud I shudder. Cam tries to rush forward to grab her but I yank the back of his shirt, pulling backward when I see the great white lion break through the trees and bound toward Maddison like his life depends on it. Fear grips me. She hasn't been able to cross that fence since she got here and now she has risked her life just to escape us. My breath lodges in my throat when she runs toward him. The lion looks angry and ready to shred anything in his path and I worry she has mistaken his love for her.

I force myself to not look away, if that fucking beast is going to take her from me then I won't look away and leave her alone in her last moments.

Cam is stiff and taut as he stands beside me, watching with bated breath to see what the fuck Hades is going to do. When the lion slides to a stop in front of her, I stop breathing. Maddison runs her fingers through his mane, then runs past him. The lion looks directly at us, then bares his teeth before following his master into the woods where we can't follow.

"How the fuck do we get to her?" Cam utters with an edge to his voice.

A sigh pushes its way past my lips as I scrub a hand down my face. "We don't." He whirls around and pins me with a glare.

"I'm not leaving her out there," he snarls.

I reach out and place a hand on his shoulder. He smacks it away, then shoves me back a step. I bite the inside of my cheek to keep myself from lashing out at him. I know Cameron is in love with her, which is the only reason he is getting a free pass right now.

"She went to Hades because she knows we *can't* follow, Cameron. She wants to be left alone and there is nothing we can do right now short of sedating the lion, but I don't like our chances of her forgiving us for doing that."

His face falls as my words sink in. "What the fuck do we do, Royce? Dad just crossed a line I don't think she will ever forgive him, or us, for." This time when I reach out and grip the back of his neck and hurl him forward until our foreheads touch, he doesn't push me away.

"We find your dad and figure out why the fuck he to lied to all of us, then we go after our girl and tell her the truth about who she has been spending her nights with."

I don't know what to think or how to feel. Hades is wrapped around me, keeping me warm and protecting me from the three guys who just ripped my world apart. I had no idea where the hell I was running to, but I just knew I needed to be somewhere I felt safe and Hades has always made me feel that way. I put my lion in a position today that I never should have, he could have turned on me because I hadn't earned his trust back. I knew in my gut that he wouldn't hurt me because Cam and Royce were right behind me and his first instinct will always be to protect those in his pride.

I lean back against him and run my hand along his fur, relishing in the feeling of having him close to me again. I never realized it until now how lost I felt without him near me. If this lion could talk he would have the power to destroy me with all the secrets I have told him. He was the first person I told about Cam and I sleeping together. He was also the first to hear me confess my attraction to Royce and Derek. I told him how I had feelings for Cam, Derek and Royce and that I was scared about how deeply I had felt for them.

"My life is a clusterfuck right now, Hades." He lets out a long yawn, earning a scowl from me. "How can you be tired right now when my life is falling apart?" The little shit flicks his tail which catches me in the side of the face. I growl and flop back against his side, loving how he grunts from the force. "Well, that will teach you not to dismiss a lady when she is having a shit time with her life," I scold him.

I know I can't stay out here all night, but the thought of having to face Joanne and watch her fawn all over Derek, while I am forced to sit there and watch has my stomach tying itself in knots. After the way he touched me and spoke to me the other night, I don't think I can go back to pretending I don't have feelings for him. Cam said that Royce and Derek feel the same way about me but they have never done anything to show me, aside from that bold move the other night, where I ran to meet my masked men so they could take the edge off.

Just the memory of what they do to me every night has me clenching my thighs together to try and dull the ache. I close my eyes and relive some of my memories of them. I love when the three of them push me to my knees and force their cocks into my mouth—

Sinner.

I jerk upright and stare wide eyed ahead as I recall memories of my masked men calling me sinner.

"Holy fuck!" I hiss into the darkness, all this time I never fucking put it together because of the fucking cock piercings. I knew Cameron and Derek never had their cocks pierced, but what if they got it done while I was gone? Or was one of those Royce's dick? No, it wasn't Royce's because I saw his when Cameron was on his knees blowing him. "It's them," I breathe out, that's why they never came to the rescue when I screamed for them.

Holy shit.

I may be pissed off and angry with Derek but I want to know. No, I *need* to know the truth. I turn and run a hand through my boy's mane, then place a kiss on the side of his face.

"Wish me luck, I'm about to go and turn some lives upside down, but I promise I'll never leave you again, Hades," I vow, then make my way out of the woods. My anxiety has me in a chokehold and nerves are strangling the air from my lungs. Confronting the three of them and accusing them of being the three masked men that have been fucking me every single night is a huge risk.

What if I'm wrong?

The thought hits me with so much power that I slam to a halt. What if I am wrong and I go in there accusing them of wearing masks while they fuck me and I'm not right?

The thought vanishes from my mind when I see a lone figure against the fence. I nibble my lip nervously. I square my shoulders and hold my head high as I make my way toward him. The moon offers enough light for me to see who it is as I draw near. It surprises me when I see it isn't Cameron waiting for me.

"Sinner." Royce's gruff tone washes over me as I stop a few feet away from the fence. Royce's gaze darts over my shoulder and I know without needing to look that Hades is coming.

"What are you doing here?" I ask.

He releases a breath and stabs a hand through his hair. I can see he is clearly uncomfortable about something but I refuse to fill the silence. "Cam and I had no idea that Derek was still in contact with your mother." The truth is clear in his words and knowing that him and Cameron didn't betray me has some of the tension fleeing my body.

"Is that the only reason you're out here?" I push.

His gaze locks with mine and I can see a range of emotions swirling in the depths of those brown eyes. "No. I've been out here for hours waiting for you."

"Why?"

"Because I needed to know you were safe and that we wouldn't lose you again." His raw honesty has my breath hitching. "Maddison, I don't want you to run again. You belong here with us and I know Derek doing what he did hurt you, but I would be a liar if I said I wasn't grateful that he had a way to get in contact with Joanne."

"He lied to me!" I snap.

Royce nods and smiles sadly. "I know he did and he has a lot of explaining to do, but if there is a chance he can get her to confess and grant you your freedom, then I'm all for it."

"Why do you care so much about me going to

prison?" I press, needing to hear his answer. I try not to sound too hopeful but I fail.

His eyes take on an intense look as he stares at me. "Because you're ours and your place is here with us, not in some cell or a shitty apartment hours away. You belong to us." My jaw unhinges, words fail me. I don't know what to say or what to do, I just stand here staring at him, wondering if I'm dreaming or if this is really happening.

"Royce—"

He cuts me off before I can finish. "I can see the questions you have for us in your eyes but I can't answer them without my brother or Cam, so I'm begging you to come back to the house with me so we have a chance to explain everything before you write us off and run."

"I never said I was gonna run," I whisper.

The smile falls from his face. "You might when you learn everything," he mutters.

I press forward and grip the fence. He reaches out and places his fingers over mine, drawing a gasp from me. "I don't want to run, I want to fight," I admit quietly.

"Then let us fight beside you. I swear, sinner, we won't let you go without a fight. Have faith in us."

"I'm not religious, Royce."

He smirks and shoots me a wink as he steps back motioning to the gate. "I know but you should start praying because when the truth comes out only God will be able to save you from what is in store for you and that perfect little body."

Oh shit, I was right. They are my masked men.

EIGHTEEN
DEREK

Standing here in the middle of my living room, facing the woman who is soon to be my ex-wife has disgust rolling through me. Joanne looks nothing like her daughter. Her scraggly brown hair looks like a bird's nest atop her head, her dull brown eyes are void of life and wonder. She is far too skinny and her bones protrude, that's what happens when you abuse drugs. I sneer at her best friend Scarlet, who is practically a carbon copy of Maddison's mother. How this woman was able to give life to the most perfect creature I have ever laid eyes on is a mystery to me.

"So, where is the disappointment?" Joanne rasps out, her voice croaky and sounds like a pack a day smoker.

"The only disappointment here is you," Cameron snaps from beside me.

Joanne flicks her gaze to my son and smiles, showcasing her missing front teeth. "Is that any way to speak to your mother?" she volleys back.

Now I growl, drawing her attention back to me. "You are nothing to my son," I force out through clenched teeth.

She waves me off. "You promised me money if I came here and saw her. Now where is the money?" This fucking woman is one of a kind.

"Do you even care that you've hurt your daughter?" Cam snarls, not giving her a chance to answer before pushing on. "Maddison is fucking incredible. She's smart and funny. She is beautiful and has the most amazing personality and the biggest heart."

"And your point is?' she fires back with an edge to her tone.

"His point is that your daughter is fucking perfect, yet she has a mother who cares for no one but herself," I spit out.

"She was a mistake I should have swallowed." Anger surges through me at her reply. I open my mouth ready to rip her a new one but clamp it closed when Royce suddenly appears at my other side. I watch as my dirty little sinner comes around him and stands in front of the three of us, facing off against her mother and the bitch that sold her out.

"Mother," Maddison snarls that one word with so much hatred.

Joanne and Scarlet both scowl at my girl and it hits me then, they hate Maddy because they are jealous of her.

"Say what it is you wanted to say so I can get my money and leave." Maddy stiffens at her mother's words. I place my hand against her lower back, offering her my silent support. Cam steps up to her side and interlocks his fingers with hers, at his touch she relaxes. Joanne glares at their joined hand. "Oh, that is fucking rich. You judge me, yet here you are whoring yourself out to your brother." Scarlet and her laugh but Maddy doesn't cower.

"Least I know the name of the guy sliding his cock inside me." At her retort I bite down on my lip to keep from laughing, the humor isn't lost on Royce who shakes with silent laughter.

"Hurry up, girl, I don't have time for your drama. I got things to do," Scarlet hisses, earning a glare from me and the guys.

Maddy scoffs. "I didn't call you here."

Joanne frowns at her, then darts her gaze to me. "What the fuck is this, Derek?" she barks.

"This is the part where I tell you that your endless stream of money has run out," I answer. Her face pales and she places her hand over her heart, like I just ripped the fucking thing out. I can feel Maddy, Cam and Royce all looking at me, but I keep my focus on the bitch. "You won't receive another dime from me. I paid you to leave her the fuck alone but you didn't listen, did you?"

"What the fuck, Dad?" Cam's question is ignored when Joanne answers.

"I never went near the bitch—"

I cut her off. "You didn't, but your side piece did and you used her name and address to get her arrested. I won't let her go to jail for you."

"You can't do shit, Derek!" she screams.

I smile cruelly as I meet her deranged gaze. "I already have." Joanne stumbles back a step. When her eyes harden and I see nothing but deep hatred in her soulless eyes, I know she is going to blow my world apart and tell them my deepest, darkest secret.

"You rat me out and I'll tell them that you paid me for her," she sneers. Maddison, Royce and Cam all spin around to face me. I ignore my brother and son as I focus on Maddison, her eyes wide and filled with confusion as she stares up at me.

"What is she talking about?" she breathes out.

"When I first met her she came here to meet someone. She had planned to sell you to him." Maddison's face pales as her eyes widen in shock at my declaration. "When I found out what she was doing, I offered her another solution."

"You paid for me?" Her eyes are filled with devastation and her tone is laced with anguish.

I shake my head. "No. She told me the only way to stop the deal was for me to marry her. I had to pay her monthly and make sure the money never stopped or she would... use you against me."

"Why the hell would you care about someone you didn't even know?" she bites out.

I take a deep breath and force myself to admit the truth. "The truth is that night none of us had seen Joanne, only you. You captured my son's attention instantly when he saw you getting off the ferris wheel. Then Royce spotted you at the cotton candy stand and couldn't keep his eyes off you, but then you walked right past me and stole the breath from my lungs." Tears fill her eyes at my revelation. "I followed you. When I saw you talking to Joanne I decided to approach her and ask about you and that's when she told me about her plan. I should have walked away and kept my nose out of it, but when Royce and Cameron told me they spotted this girl and we all realized we were transfixed on the same person, I couldn't turn away."

"You married her for... me?" she whispers brokenly.

I nod. "I paid her more money to leave and never come back after a couple of months. She was all too happy to accept the cash and vanish. When you left, I reached out to her and told her as long as she stayed away from you the money would keep coming, but she broke the deal and now, she will be left with nothing."

"You can't fucking do that. I'll go to the cops," Joanne screams. "I'll tell them how you used my daughter against me—"

"Shut the fuck up, you washed up whore. No one would shed a tear if you dropped dead right now," Royce snarls.

"No need to call the cops, they are waiting outside for you." Joanne's eyes pop wide. Scarlet darts across the room to peer out the window and curses.

"The pigs are right there, Jo," Scarlet hisses.

"What the fuck have you done?" Joanne roars.

I tear my gaze from Maddison to look at her mother. "I made sure you finally pay for your crimes. The sheriff is a buddy of mine and I made sure to show him my bank records of all the payments I made to you as proof. He also has Maddison's statements from her previous arrests as proof that you set her up. The only reason they couldn't drop the charges is because you were never found. But now, they have no choice but to take her statements seriously because you're here and I hope you fucking rot in prison for the rest of your miserable life, you bitch."

Everything is a blur. I just stand still as the sheriff cuffs my mom and leads her out of here, kicking and screaming. Turns out Scarlet has warrants and is arrested with my mom. The sheriff told me he would be in contact in regard to my court case and has high hopes that the case will be thrown out. The relief I expect to feel over the news never comes, all I feel is confusion. I can't handle being in the same room as all of them, so I escape to my room, needing time to process everything I have just learned.

I thought they never saw me like I saw them, but it turns out, they saw me first. Cam was right, Royce and Derek do have feelings for me and I was just too blinded to see it. The night Royce and Cam walked in on me sucking Derek off I thought he didn't know it was me, now I'm not so sure that was the case.

All these questions are swirling through my mind and I have no way to answer them. Royce promised me answers earlier at Hades enclosure.

"Goddamnit, Maddison, put your big girl pants on and get your ass downstairs and demand answers!" I scold myself. I creep out of my room and keep my head held high as I make my way downstairs. I frown when I don't see anyone in the living room. "Hello?" I call out, it's late so I know they won't be working. My train of thought is derailed when the room is suddenly bathed in darkness. My heart begins pounding inside my chest. I close my eyes and strain my hearing, footsteps sounding throughout the room. I blink my eyes open and gasp at the sight of blue, red and yellow standing before me with only the light from their masks illuminating the space.

I study them and take in their attire and the way they all stand and I now know for certain I was right. How I didn't put it together sooner is a fucking mystery to me.

"Are you ready?" yellow asks in his robotic voice.

"Ready for what?" I reply.

"To know the truth," blue answers.

"What if I already know?" I volley back.

"Then there is no longer any use for these," red says, then reaches up and removes his mask. I may have known I was right, but thinking it and seeing it are two different things. I watch yellow and blue remove their masks. Cam rushes off somewhere while I stand here staring at the other two. When the lights suddenly come on, I have to close my eyes to adjust. As I slowly blink them open, Cam saunters back into the room and stands beside his father. Silence stretches between us as we just look at each other.

"We had no right wanting you," Royce says, his words have a pang hitting me in the chest.

"We should have done the right thing and left you alone to live your life," Derek adds.

"But, we couldn't live without you and this house isn't a home without you in it," Cameron tacks on, causing tears to spring to my eyes.

"From the moment I saw you, I knew you would change all of our lives." Royce's tone holds an edge of longing.

"We belong to you, sinner." Cam's words hold such conviction I actually believe him.

"You're ours and even if you try to fight this, we'll fight back harder than ever to prove to you that we are the only men in this world that can handle your urges and wants. We'll love you harder than you have ever been loved, and we will remind you daily that you are wanted and cherished because that's what it's like to be owned by us." Derek's admission has my heart beating so fast and the blood rushing south, causing a throbbing ache to make itself known between my legs. "You can either surrender and allow us to show you how we feel about you, or you can play hard to get and fight this. But we will chase your ass down and drag you back here by your hair and punish your pussy for denying us what's *ours*."

My breaths are coming out in fast pants, my questions I needed answers to minutes ago have vanished and replaced with raw carnal need for the three of them. To finally see their faces and know they have been the ones behind the masks this whole time adds a new level of seduction to this moment. I could run and have them chase me, knowing they love to hunt me as much as I love to run, but not tonight. All I want is for them to take me and mark me as theirs. All the questions can wait until morning because tonight, I just need my guys.

I grip the hem of my shirt and love the way they track my every movement as I slowly lift it over my head and toss it to the side. The groans that escape them at the sight of my bare chest has me biting back a smile. I went braless today and I'm grateful for that choice. I pop the button on my pants and slowly drag the zipper down, drawing this out. When I slowly begin pushing them down my legs, Cam lifts his fist to his mouth and bites down on it. I kick them to the side and I stand before them in nothing but my black thong.

The heated look in their eyes sends a shiver down my spine. Being able to see their faces only serves to enhance my need. Most would feel betrayed over them lying to me for weeks, but I don't. All I feel is gratification that they found a way to be with me.

"I'm yours," I say huskily, the sound of my voice seems to be what snaps them out of their trance. The three of them rush toward me and form a semicircle with Derek standing directly in front of me. He reaches out and cups my cheeks tenderly between his hands as Royce kneels down and slides my thong down my legs, exposing my pussy. Derek captures my lips in a heated kiss as I feel Cam's fingers slide through my folds. I gasp into Derek's mouth when I feel Royce part my cheeks. A second later I cry out as his tongue prods my muscle wall but Derek swallows the sound.

Cam pushes two fingers inside me and I nearly come on the spot.

I reach up and lock my arms around Derek's neck, trying to deepen the kiss but he jerks back and glares down at me. "You don't get to fucking touch." I close my eyes and savor the sound of his voice. Many nights I had imagined their voices instead of the robotic ones and now I finally get to hear their true tones, and it sends a shiver down my spine. I cry out when Cam curls his fingers and strokes that sweet spot inside me as Royce pushes his tongue inside me.

"You have no fucking idea how hard I am for you right now," Cam growls. I peer up at him with longing in my eyes. He curses, then seals his lips to mine, tasting me. Knowing I just had his father's tongue down my throat and now his has a thrill going through me.

"Enough!" Both Cam and Royce instantly obey and I whimper as they remove their fingers and tongue. I shoot Derek a glare, which only earns me a dark look. He yanks his hoodie off and exposes his naked chest and I fight not to moan at the sight. I dart my gaze either side of me and watch both Cam and Royce begin to undress. When they all stand before me naked and erect, I smile at the sight of the piercings on Derek and Cam's cocks.

Not needing to be prompted I lower to my knees and stare up at Royce as I wrap my lips around his dick. I reach out and grip Cam, loving the sound of the hiss that escapes him. It takes Derek a minute before he is standing at my other side. I grab him in my free hand, then switch to sucking Cam off while jerking Derek and Royce off.

The feeling of her hot mouth wrapped around me is a feeling I will never tire of. She is a fucking goddess, the way she can take us and submit to our will only turns us all on more. She is perfect. She releases me with a wet pop before replacing her mouth with her hand and blowing my dad. The fucker tangles his fingers in her hair and takes control as he thrusts inside her mouth, causing her to gag around him, but he doesn't slow his pace, knowing she can handle it. The sounds she makes has me reaching for Royce. I grip the back of his neck and pull his mouth to mine.

Royce opens for me instantly and moans into my mouth, being able to have him and Maddison together is a dream come true. We may not be in a committed relationship, but Royce and I love fucking each other and I never want that to stop. We'll pledge ourselves to her but we'll never stop burying our cocks inside each other, plus we know she gets off on watching us.

"Fuck," Dad roars. Royce and I break apart to see him jerk backward. He uses his hold on her hair to pull her to her feet. Maddy whimpers but doesn't protest as he drags her toward the sofa. Dad drops down onto the sofa and stares up at her with a dark look in his eyes. "Fuck me, sinner." She eagerly scrambles onto his lap and lines him up with her entrance before slowly sinking down onto him.

"Holy fuck," she breathes out when he's sheathed inside her but she doesn't move, she peers over her shoulder at us and smirks. "Royce I want you in my ass while Cam fucks you." Royce chuckles and makes his way over to her. He runs his hand down her naked back then reaches around and grips her chin, forcing her head back. She opens her mouth for him. He spits in her mouth, then slaps her. She moans which only has him repeating the move. She begins bouncing up and down on Dad as I slip behind Royce.

He pushes her forward so she is flat against Dad, then spits on his hand and lathers his cock. "No lube tonight, baby. I'm taking this ass raw and you are going to fucking love it."

"Yes, Royce," she begs a second before she kisses Dad and grinds against him. Royce spreads her cheeks and lines himself up. She goes tense but then Dad jerks inside her, distracting her from Royce sliding inside her tight ass. I force Royce forward and repeat his move. I spit on my hand and ease inside him. Unlike him, I don't go slow to not cause Maddy any harm. I slam inside him, relishing the pained snarl that rips out of him as he slams forward inside her, causing her to scream out. Unable to control myself I draw back and thrust forward, causing the three of them to weather the brunt of my force and loving the sounds that they make.

"Fuck, your cunt is strangling my cock," Dad grits out.

"You feel so good inside me." Our dirty little sinner moans as she tries to take control, but I refuse to allow her as I slam forward, forcing her to submit to me. Royce grips her hair and tugs her head to the side, then claims her lips. Dad cups her tits and pinches her nipples, and a strangled sound escapes her when dad bites down on the soft flesh between her neck and shoulder.

Royce breaks the kiss and looks back at me. "I

want my dick in her mouth when I come." I grin and nod, knowing what Royce means is he wants to come all over her face, lick it off, then spit it in her mouth.

He gets off on the taste of his own cum.

"Oh God, I need more, please!" Maddy cries out.

"You want it hard and rough, baby?" Dad growls.

"Yes. I need it," she begs. I pull out of Royce and step aside, giving him space. He eases out of her, spins around and moves the coffee table to the side. Dad lifts her off him, then she turns to me with a hungry look in her eyes. I reach out and grip her waist, lifting her. She locks her legs around me, then bends down and kisses me. I growl my approval as I slowly pull her to the rug. She opens her legs wide and I slide inside her tight little cunt with ease. She arches her back off the ground. I swallow her cries of pleasure as I thrust inside her hard, making sure she can feel every fucking inch of me.

"Take every fucking thing he gives you like a good little slut," Royce hisses. The need to come overwhelms me and I can't stop myself. The second I feel her pussy clamp down on me as her orgasm rocks through her with the rage of an erupting volcano, I cum deep inside her. Shudders roll through the both of us. I barely have a second to catch my breath before I'm yanked off her and my dad is claiming my spot. Not one to be left out, Royce straddles her face and shoves his cock down her throat as Dad slams inside her.

I lean back against the sofa utterly sated and now that the haze of sexual tension has been eased, I feel like I can focus. Maddy is gagging and trying to pull back from Royce but he won't allow it. He presses forward onto his hands and knees and begins fucking her mouth like a savage.

Dad lifts her legs and throws them over his shoulders, giving him better access. I smirk at the thought of my dad blowing his load inside her, mixing his cum with mine. His could have been siblings and mine could have been grandkids.

"Fuck, just like that, sinner," Royce shouts, his thrusts turning erratic as his climax draws near. Four more thrusts, then he is pulling out of her. She gasps and sucks in lungfuls of air as Royce pumps himself in his hand. "Mouth open now, you dirty bitch." She obeys and pokes her tongue out just in time for the first stream of cum to hit her face. Royce throws his head back, roaring her name as he comes all over her face. Dad hasn't eased up and Maddy is squirming with need. Royce hops off her, then bends down and licks the cum from her face.

"Don't you fucking come!" Dad warns.

"Please," Maddy screams as Royce spits his cum into her mouth, then forces her mouth closed. When she swallows, he releases his hold and smiles down at her.

"Good girl." His praise sends a shiver through her. With him out of the way, Dad pushes forward, pressing her knees against her chest as he fucks her.

"Oh shit, you're so fucking deep, Derek," she screams. Dad continues to fuck her like a savage, the sight alone has me getting hard and without thought I grip the back of Royce's neck and force his mouth onto my cock. The second I feel his tongue swirl around the base I groan, drawing Maddy's attention to us.

"You like watching that?" Dad presses.

"Yes, I fucking love it," she answers between moans. Royce sucks my cock like a pro and I know with how turned on I am I won't last long. I fight off the urge to explode in his mouth, needing to come with Maddy. I see tears rolling down her cheeks and know she is fighting not to come or she risks my dad's ire.

"Fuck yes, this pussy is mine, sinner," he roars.

"It's yours, now please let me come," she begs.

"Come for me, my little sinner," he urges. On the next thrust, Maddison comes so fucking hard her whole body turns red from the pressure of her release, and her screams echo through the house. Dad slams inside her, chasing his own release, but I beat him to it. I tangle my hand in Royce's hair and hold him there as I come down his throat with her name on my lips. Dad follows me over the cliff seconds later. Royce rips free of my cock, then spins around, grips her chin and forces her mouth open, and spits my cum into her mouth.

"Round one done," Dad says after he regains his composer and pulls out of her. Maddy stares up at him with wide eyes.

"What?" she balks.

"We own a carnival and we plan to fuck you on every single one of the rides, but for tonight, we'll be gentleman and let you choose if we should chase you through the maze or the haunted house?" Her eyes are as wide as saucers as she looks at me. I decide to be kind and offer her another option. "Or, you can sit on my cock on the pirate ship, fuck Royce on the ferris wheel and then let my dad finger you on the rollercoaster. Which one do you choose?"

The past six months have been a dream.

I have been living on cloud nine and waiting to wake up from this dream of a place but I won't, because this is my reality.

This is my life.

I wake up every morning to three men who treat me like a fucking queen. They dote on me and everywhere I am you can expect to find one of them with me, always. Well, except for when I'm with Hades, that is the one place they can't follow me. I know it drives them insane when I lose track of time with him and they can't just come and get me, but I refuse to leave my boy out.

We have another lion coming in next weekend, a female who was used in a breeding ring and treated badly. She is weary of humans and known to attack, but that didn't stop me from agreeing to take her. I had an enclosure set up for her beside Hades and my hope is that he will find a friend in her and not have to be out here on his own anymore. I tried to convince the guys to let me bring him in the house, but the three of them vetoed my idea. I even tried to fuck a yes out of them but apparently the potential of being ripped apart by a lion was greater.

Joanne was charged three months ago and sentenced. All charges against me have been dropped and my name is now cleared. Derek and Royce pushed both me and Cam to study. I refused to go away to college, though Cam was all for the idea because he said he would get unlimited time alone with me. I smile at the thought of him, he is the sweetest guy and always knows how to cheer me up. Royce is the one who pushes me and refuses to allow me to settle. Derek on the other hand, he demands me to take control of my life and not get lost in them.

I'm studying zoology and Cam is studying to become a structural engineer. He and I spend our days taking online classes and studying until Royce and Derek get home, and that's when the real fun begins. For the past six months I haven't had a single night where one of them wasn't inside me.

Most guys hate the idea of women on their periods, but not my guys. Royce loves the taste of my blood and Derek loves smearing it all over me before we fuck. Cam loves how wet it makes me feel and every month, it's like a beast replaces each of them during that week. They are ravenous and fight each other to get to me.

Next year we plan to go on vacation over the winter to Switzerland, where we can ski and hang out in a log cabin and get lost in each other.

"Sinner." I lift my gaze from my laptop to see Royce and Derek standing at the end of the table with sinister looks in their eyes. I turn to my side to look at Cam, only to find him smirking at me.

"What's going on?" I ask warily.

"We have a new attraction," Royce answers.

"Okayyyyyy." I'm still not following.

"It's called the tower of terror," Derek says.

"And what does that have to do with me?" I run my gaze over each of them, waiting for a response.

"We all have a bet going on to see who can make you come on the ride. Whoever makes you come first gets you to themselves for two days." I balk at Cameron.

"I'm not a prize to be won," I hiss.

"Of course not, baby. We won you years ago.

Now get the fuck up, you dirty little sinner, and get your ass over here because tonight, we're going to see how much of a slut you really are and how much you can take before we break you." Derek's dirty promise has me clenching my thighs together.

Forgive me Mother, for I love living in sin and will gladly buy a first class ticket to hell if it means I get to keep riding on the three of them.

Do you still have a fear of clowns after knowing how good they fuck?
I hope not because hot fucking damn, Daddy and his boys had me panting!
Thank you so much for reading Dirty Little Sinner, I fucking loved writing this book, truly. I have always wanted to write a pure smut book and I finally got the chance to do that.

I cannot thank you enough for reading *Dirty Little Sinner*, it means the world to me that you have taken a chance on reading one of my books!
If you would leave a review that would be amazing!

Newsletter 
Facebook 
Reader's Group 
Instagram 
TikTok 
Amazon 
Website 
Bookbub 🤍
Goodreads 🤍
Linktree 🤍

ACKNOWLEDGMENTS

Marcus, my dirty little sinner. Thank you for allowing me to wear a mask and chase you around and take you however and whenever I wanted. I loved getting to call you my dirty little whore, that shit had me panting.

MJ & Ray-Ray, my loves. I pray to God that you both never read this acknowledgment because then that means you read this book and fuck that. This book is not for you, my darlings. Please forgive Mummy for being a dirty little sinner.

Leah, my dark and depraved Wednesday Adams. I could not have done any of this without you, babe. I love you and I am so grateful for you every single day.

My PA, Sarah–My Queen–Wilson. I don't know how I got so lucky with you! This whole author thing would suck without you by my side. You are worth your weight in gold, my queen.

My alpha's: Debbie, Clare, Erin and Samantha (number 2). You ladies are the best fucking people I know and I wouldn't be able to put these books out without you. Thank you from the bottom of my heart for following me on this crazy as fuck journey.

My beta babes: Taay, Amber, Amanda, Nicole, Patti, Morgan & Rizzo. I fucking love you crazy ladies. Thank you for being on this dirty ass ride with me.

My ARC army girls. Thank you beautiful souls so fucking much for always sticking by me and trusting me to mend those hearts that I break.

Lizz, you are the backbone to this operation and without you we would all fall. Thank you for not only being my editor but my friend and for always giving me the best advice.

My darling dark delicious readers. Thank you again for following me and reading each of these books. I cannot tell you how much it means to me that you follow me on this ride and love each of these characters as much as I do.

Sam xxx

Mafia Romance's

https://books.bookfunnel.com/mafiaseries

Secret Society/ Bully/ Masked Men

https://books.bookfunnel.com/ dirtytemptation

Sinners Welcome (Pure Smut Novellas)

https://books.bookfunnel.com/ sinnerswelcome

Samantha's Entire Backlist

https://books.bookfunnel.com/ SamanthasBookverse

ABOUT THE AUTHOR

Samantha Barrett is originally from Auckland, New Zealand but living in Brisbane, Australia.

Sam writes all things dirty, dark and delicious with a side of twisted mind fuck.

She is a lover of all things red flags and an anti-hero is a must.

9 781764 107693